D0771419

THE CARETAKER'S
GUIDE TO
FABLEHAVEN

THE CARETAKER'S GUIDE TO FABLEHAVEN

WRITTEN BY

BRANDON MULL

ILLUSTRATIONS BY

BRANDON DORMAN

WITHDRAWN

SHADOW
MOUNTAIN

EST. 1711

Backgrounds throughout the book from Shutterstock.com: © javarman, © khz, © KN, © REDAV, © design36, © kzww, © Nella, © Lora liu, © Oleg Golovnev, © M. Unal Ozmen, © revers, © Ivankov, Hobort, © Kidsana Maimeetook.

Text © 2015 Creative Concepts, LC

Illustrations © 2015 Brandon Dorman

All rights reserved. No part of this book may be reproduced in any form or by any means without permission in writing from the publisher, Shadow Mountain®, at permissions@shadowmountain.com or P.O. Box 30178, Salt Lake City, Utah 84130. The views expressed herein are the responsibility of the author and do not necessarily represent the position of Shadow Mountain.

All characters in this book are fictitious, and any resemblance to actual persons, living or dead, is purely coincidental.

Visit us at ShadowMountain.com

Library of Congress Cataloging-in-Publication Data

Mull, Brandon, 1974- author.

 The caretaker's guide to Fablehaven / Brandon Mull ; illustrations by Brandon Dorman.

      pages cm

 Summary: An encyclopedia of the creatures, characters, artifacts, items, and places found in the Fablehaven series.

  ISBN 978-1-62972-091-3 (hardbound : alk. paper)

[1. Fantasy.] I. Dorman, Brandon, illustrator. II. Title.

 PZ7.M9112Car 2015

 [Fic]—dc23   2015010148

Printed in China   05/2015
RR Donnelley, Shenzhen, China

10 9 8 7 6 5 4 3 2 1

To Brandon Dorman, who gives
Fablehaven such a distinctive look.

And to all others who have cared about Fablehaven!
—BRANDON MULL

For Dan Burr, the Jedi Master.
—BRANDON DORMAN

CONTENTS

Introduction Page ❦ viii

Artifacts & Items Page ❦ 1

Creatures Page ❦ 19

Demons Page ❦ 65

Dragons Page ❦ 77

Locations Page ❦ 87

Wizards Page ❦ 109

Index Page ❦ 113

INTRODUCTION

If you are in possession of this book you are assumed to be the caretaker or an apprentice caretaker of Fablehaven. By now you've been introduced to the world of mythical and magical creatures. However, there is still much to learn. Previous caretakers of Fablehaven thought it would be helpful to create a *Caretaker's Guide* specifically for those tasked with the job of nurturing, protecting, and surviving this preserve and its inhabitants.

Do not be fooled. Fablehaven is an unpredictable and dangerous place. However, the collective knowledge gathered within the pages of this bestiary will give you the tools needed not only to survive but to thrive.

The creatures of Fablehaven are either light or dark, not necessarily good or evil. In order to be good, one must recognize the difference between right and wrong and strive to choose the right. To be truly evil one must do the contrary. Being good or evil is a choice. This is often not so with the creatures of Fablehaven. Their fundamental natures largely govern how they act. Some are inherently builders, some are nurturers, some are playful. Some are inherently destroyers, some are deceivers, some crave power. Some love light, some love darkness. But change their natures and, without much resistance, their identities follow. Like a fairy becoming an imp, or an imp regaining her fairyhood.

Much counsel and advice has been passed down over the generations. Want to know what most caretakers agree is the most invaluable tip? Those who are careful to cause no mischief, work no magic, and inflict no harm are protected by the foundational treaty of Fablehaven. This truth can be your strongest ally and at times your only defense.

One final note. The signs leading up to the front gate were not always there. In the late eighteenth century, before the guest register that controls access to Fablehaven was created, two poachers entered the property in search of big game. Needless to say, they found it. Or it found them. Many days later, the resident caretaker found them as well. Or at least he found the stony remains of their petrified bodies. And thus the first signs outside the gates of Fablehaven were posted.

As caretaker you have accepted a most noble assignment. Keep your eyes open. Obey with exactness. Take risks only as a last resort, and you will have a better chance at seeing another sunrise.

Welcome to Fablehaven.

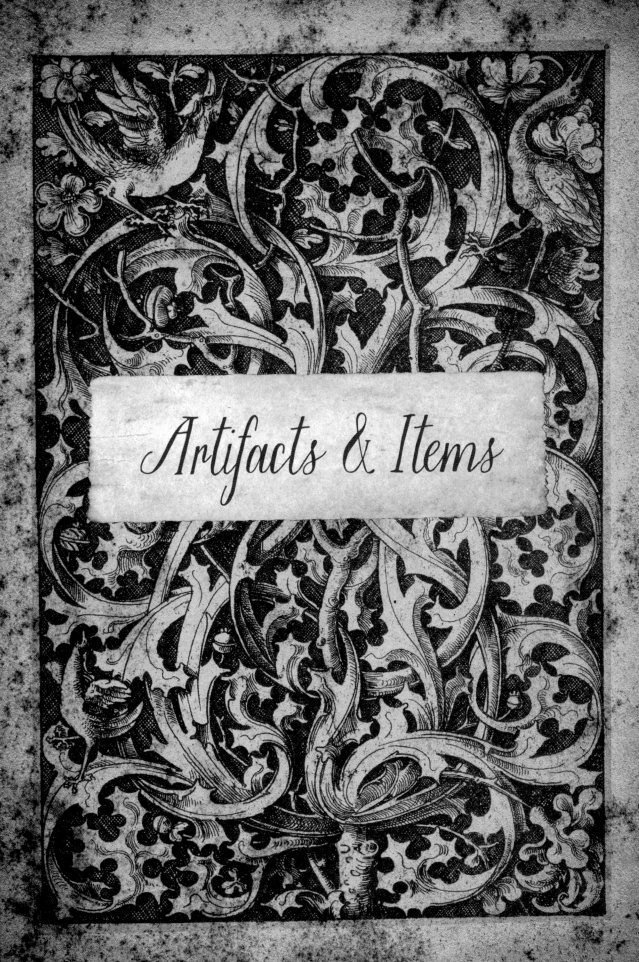

Artifacts & Items

ADAMANT BREASTPLATE

This smoky-gray breastplate is a priceless, supernaturally durable piece of armor. It is made from adamant, the lightest yet strongest spell-forged metal alloy, which means it can't be bent or broken, and is impenetrable. It will stop any blade, turn any arrow, and can even hold up under the force of a sledgehammer. The breastplate is a coveted item and wealthy lords have been known to empty their treasuries to acquire it.

It is believed that the priceless armor is somewhere on the preserve. The last report mentioned a fog giant using it like a skipping stone. He was last glimpsed with it somewhere in Kurisock's domain.

Satyrs retrieved it from the tar pits.

LUCK
· · · · · · · · · · · ·
HAS A WAY
—OF—
evaporating
when you
LEAN ON IT.
—WARREN

ANTI-EAVESDROPPING CANDLE

This protective item allows a private conversation to remain confidential. As this fat white candle burns, it prevents any outsider from overhearing sensitive information.

Extra candles can be found in the wooden cabinet in the hidden attic.

BOTTLED MESSAGES

Messages can be delivered in the form of a green glass bottle. When the bottle's cork is removed, a colored gas is released and takes the shape of the message bearer, who then delivers the message in the form of a "talking letter."

To record your message, simply uncork the bottle and speak into the colored gas as it is released. Remember, you *must* speak the name of the recipient as the message will not be delivered unless the intended person is in the room and can identify himself or herself.

Once the message is finished, tap the top of the bottle three times. The colored gas will be sucked back into the bottle along with everything you communicated. Quickly recork the bottle.

There is a set of ~~six~~ bottles on the top shelf of the wooden cabinet in the secret attic ready to record your letters.

FIVE. One used by Patton Burgess

Very disappointing if you're thirsty. S.S.

I agree times ten! —Newel

Who let the satyr make notes in here? K.S.

DISTRACTER SPELL

Fairykind are immune to this spell!

Fablehaven is surrounded by a distracter spell—a form of mind control that diverts one's focus away from a protected object or area. This powerful enchantment is often used to protect magical preserves from mortals or other unwanted visitors.

DRAGON TEARS

Dragons have made me cry! Grrr... K.S.

A much-sought-after, potent ingredient for making potions, dragon tears are extremely difficult to come by because dragons only weep when they are in the deepest of mourning or if they have committed a terrible betrayal. Dragon tears cannot be faked or forced, and so cruel people have been known to capture a young dragon and murder its family just to collect its tears.

EYE DROPS

When applied to a person's eyes, these magically enhanced drops will allow the individual to see mystical creatures as they truly appear. The drops burn like acid when they are first applied. *Located in medicine cabinet, master bathroom*

FLASH POWDER

A volatile, glittery dust that crackles, sizzles, and creates a blinding flash when hurled into the air. Useful as a defense against dark powers. Fablehaven caretakers can find a small barrel of flash powder in the secret attic.

HOLLY WAND

Aholly wand is a short, crooked stick that, when held above the head, wards off phantoms. The inherent properties of holly are a natural repellent for phantoms and ghosts.

Holly supplier— Coulter Dixon

Not the best item but better than nothing! S.S.

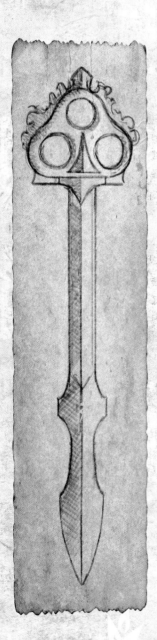

KEY TO THE INVERTED TOWER

This six-foot-long key sports a complicated series of protuberances and notches and can be used to open a long, cylindrical set of stairs that leads to the bottom of the inverted tower at Fablehaven.

The socket for the key is found at the center of a circular platform with concentric grooves radiating out from the center like the rings around a bull's-eye. When the key is first inserted into the center platform's notch, each concentric ring drops away in sequence until a conical stairway is formed, leading to the floor of the chamber. When the key is withdrawn, the portion with the notches and protuberances will separate from the rest, leaving behind a slender, double-edged spearhead.

KEYS TO ZZYZX

Located on the Shoreless Isle somewhere in the Atlantic, Zzyzx was designed to be an impenetrable prison for evil demons. The only way to access this prison is to acquire the five ancient artifacts/keys. One of those keys is hidden at Fablehaven. (*See also* Zzyzx.)

MANY LIVES WERE LOST TO
PROTECT THESE ARTIFACTS.

MAY THEY FOREVER BE
HIDDEN FROM THOSE WITH
EVIL INTENTIONS.

Patton can work it better than we can.
—K.S.

CHRONOMETER

One of five hidden ancient artifacts, this golden sphere is approximately one foot in diameter, has a polished surface interrupted by several dials and buttons, and is reputed to be the most complicated artifact to use. The Chronometer controls time in various ways, though the precise settings for any endeavor can be difficult to ascertain. Not only can the artifact speed up or slow down time, it can also move people or objects through time within certain limits. The Chronometer was originally hidden at Lost Mesa but was eventually moved to Fablehaven.

FONT OF IMMORTALITY

The Font of Immortality consists of an alabaster goblet embellished with gold and shimmering enamel. The straight, pearly spiral of a unicorn horn serves as its stem, and a sturdy base finishes it off. This gilded goblet grants immortality to the person who drinks from it at least once a week. If the Font is ever broken, it will re-form and appear somewhere else.

OCULUS

My brain has never been more fried. K.S.

Also known as the "Infinite Lens" and the "All-Seeing Eye," the Oculus is the prototype after which all seeing stones and scrying tools are patterned. This crystal artifact came from the Rio Branco preserve in Brazil and is reported to be the most dangerous of the artifacts. It allows its user to see anywhere and everywhere all at once, but most people cannot tolerate the vast and overwhelming sensory input.

SANDS OF SANCTITY

The amazing curative powers of these sands can heal seemingly irreparable wounds upon contact. Their healing powers, however, only affect the physical body, not the mind. The sands are housed in a bright copper, cat-shaped teapot.

The Sands of Sanctity—retrieved by Kendra and Seth Sorenson and company

Be careful who you heal! S.S.

TRANSLOCATOR

This artifact has power over space and can transport up to three individuals and their belongings to any place they have visited previously. The Translocator consists of a platinum cylinder set with jewels and embossed with various symbols. The cylinder is divided into three rotating sections. To activate the Translocator, the user twists the sections to bring the jewels into alignment. Each traveler then grips a different section, and the one who holds the center section controls the destination as he or she focuses on the desired location while the sections slide into place.

This was a __lifesaver__ at Wyrmroost!

KNAPSACK

Bubda Forever! S.S.

This ordinary-looking knapsack is actually an extra-dimensional storage compartment large enough to hold several people. Once a person is inside, the knapsack can be flattened, jostled, or dropped and the person will remain unaffected. (*See also* Stingbulb.)

LADY LUCK

Lady Luck is a ship with three tall masts and complex rigging, but without sails. Her wood is old and weathered but not rotten. An elaborately carved mermaid hangs at the front, face panicked, arms chained to her sides. About twenty undead, raggedly dressed deckhands man the ship.

To summon *Lady Luck,* travel to Hatteras Island, off the coast of North Carolina, and ring the bell of Cormac the leprechaun. One hundred minutes after ringing the bell, blow the whistle three times every few minutes until a rowboat arrives. Once aboard, play the music box for the presence that resides in the ship. This process secures passage to the Shoreless Isle.

The presence inside the cabin, a feminine entity who can be felt but not seen, is known to be temperamental and only respects those she fears may do her harm. Passengers cannot allow themselves to be intimidated. Also, *Lady Luck* is a one-way ship, so passengers must remember to arrange for an alternate method of return. (*See also* Leprechaun.)

MAGIC GLOVE

This fingerless leather glove renders the wearer invisible—but only when he or she holds still. The person may breathe, blink, and talk without detection, but becomes visible again once he or she moves. The glove is unable to mask smell, so some predators or enemies may not be fooled.

Current Owner is Seth Sorenson

Not as effective as flash powder, but safer to use, especially around children.

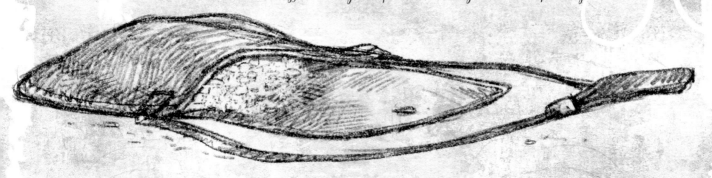

MAGIC SALT

This white powder is used to form a barrier of protection against danger, especially during Midsummer's Eve. When placed in a thick line on the floor, a goblin, for instance, will not cross it. When scattered in the air, it produces a twinkling cloud of dust particles filled with energy that repels any would-be attacker. (*See also* Flash Powder.)

PIXIE COCOON

This small, greenish pod is used by Norwegian pixies during winter hibernation. Once it has been properly treated and prepared, the pod can become an impervious shelter.

To activate this item, place it in the mouth and bite down. Almost immediately a spongy, dark cocoon will encase the user. The cocoon includes everything needed to survive for up to thirty days—even underwater. Its moist inner walls are able to filter both oxygen and carbon dioxide and are edible. The cocoon provides sustenance in the form of mildly flavored water, a gooey, peanut-butter-like matter that tastes somewhat like eggnog, and a tasteless, chewy pulp.

Although the exterior casing of the cocoon is impenetrable from the outside, one may exit by simply pushing through its walls from the inside. (*See also* Pixie.)

POTIONS

Contact Tanugatoa "Tanu" Dufu
for potion needs

The most powerful potions are made from the by-products of magical creatures, such as the milch cow, who in particular is a potion master's dream because nearly every part of the animal—milk, blood, dung, saliva, tears, and sweat—has different magical properties. (*See also* Giant Walrus; Milch Cow.)

Magical ingredients can come from sources as diverse as fairies, wizards, dragons, and giant walruses. Because these items are often difficult and dangerous to procure, the lives of many potion masters are cut short in their quest for ingredients.

There are potions to encourage love, bravery, good cheer, and a host of other emotions. Potions can also cure illness, increase energy and alertness, awaken lost memories, and augment skills like speaking different languages, picking locks, venturing underwater, and climbing mountains.

The potions that enhance negative emotions such as fear, anger, embarrassment, and sorrow are strong but less addictive than those that enhance positive emotions such as courage, calm, confidence, and joy. Potions can throw off the natural balance of emotions if overused, and they become less potent over time, so it is important they be mixed and administered only by an expert. A few specific potions are described below.

COURAGE POTION

I'm a pro with this one. ~ S.S.

This fiery-hot liquid leaves the eyes watering and the tongue feeling like it's licked a hot iron. The initial sensation gradually fades into a warmth that spreads throughout the chest accompanied by an infusion of courage. This potion is best used when combined with a little fear and calm; otherwise, its user may become reckless and foolhardy.

ENLARGER POTION

An occasional foray into negative emotions makes feeling normal that much sweeter.
—Tanu

This concoction enables its user to double his or her height and size. The necessary ingredients are extremely difficult to obtain.

FIRE-RESISTANT POTION (DRAGON INSURANCE)

This dragon-thwarting liquid comes in small plastic cylinders topped with rubber stoppers. Though not completely fire*proof*, the user of this potion becomes fire resistant, which is useful when confronting fire-breathing creatures. Sweet, spicy, cool, and tangy as it is swallowed, this concoction also provides some protection against electricity and includes a jolt of courage to help combat dragon terror.

GASEOUS-STATE POTION

This odiferous mixture renders its user translucent and transforms the body from a solid state into living mist. Some of the best advantages of this potion are that poison will not spread, acid cannot burn, and blood will not flow while the body is gaseous.

Seth was here! Go gaseous! Vengeful fairies can't touch you when you're a cloud! Oh, yeah!

MENTAL-PAIN POTION

Though it does no actual physical damage, this potent mixture administered by injection sends a message of extreme pain to the brain by "talking" to the nerves. The intense pain often causes the eyes to bulge, the salivary glands to become overactive, and the victim to lose consciousness.

SHRINKING POTION

Useful when the need for stealth is paramount, this potion allows the user to become eight times shorter than his or her normal height. The transformation is almost instantaneous and causes an intense tingling sensation to begin at the fingers and toes before traveling throughout the whole body. The effect lasts for about thirty minutes, but varies depending on potency.

It is important to note that this potion does not always shrink clothes, so be prepared for that beforehand. *Seth has two extra vials of shrinking potion.*

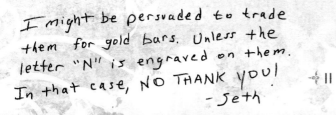

I might be persuaded to trade them for gold bars. Unless the letter "N" is engraved on them. In that case, NO THANK YOU!
—Seth

PRECIOUS FIGURINES FOUND!

Kept inside the dragon temple at Wyrmroost, this set of five statuettes is made from various precious stones: a red stone dragon, a white marble snow giant, a jade chimera, an onyx tower, and an agate leviathan.

When activated by the proper action, the potential of each figurine is revealed.

- When the red dragon is put into fire, it grows into a living dragon that will heed its master's every word.
- When buried in snow, the white marble statue expands into a mighty snow giant.
- The chimera can likewise be brought to life and is also obedient to its master's desires.
- The onyx tower, when placed on solid ground, enlarges into an actual tower.
- When dipped into the sea, the agate figurine becomes a colossal leviathan.

Seth has the tower and the leviathan figures. They may come in handy someday.

QUIET BOX

Simple and elegant, this strange, glossy black cabinet with gold trim is a miniature prison for one. The only way to release a captive from its velvety purple interior is to put another prisoner inside. It is said that the quiet box causes its prisoners to lose their grip on reality. Those placed inside can neither see, hear, nor smell anything. After a prolonged imprisonment, a captive feels unnaturally relaxed, eventually loses all sensation, and is left unable to think clearly when released.

Current prisoner of the quiet box is ... ask Seth!

RAIN STICK

This magical staff with rattles can be shaken to conjure up stormy weather, including rain, hail, thunder, and wind.

Property of Kendra Sorenson

> You see, as mortals, we can choose to break the rules. The mystical creatures that seek asylum here are not afforded that luxury. Many would break the rules if they could, but they are bound. As long as I obey the rules, I am safe. But if I lose the protections afforded by the treaty, the consequences of my vulnerability would inevitably follow.
>
> —Grandma Sorenson

SAGE'S GAUNTLETS

The wearer of these gauntlets can command dragons, and for this reason, dragons are extremely protective of them. If stolen, they will stop at nothing to retrieve them. These armored gloves are difficult to master, but the mortal who succeeds gains the ability to control dragons.

These talismans are located inside the dragon temple at Wyrmroost.

(front)   (back)

Use with crossbow

SILVER ARROW

This small arrow with its black fletching, ivory shaft, and silver arrowhead is unique because it will kill any mortal, even if he or she is enchanted or undead. In order to be effective, however, the arrow must lodge in a lethal center like the heart or brain.

SMOKE GRENADES

Filled with a purple fluid that turns to a nasty-smelling gas when exposed to air, these small glass bulbs constitute the perfect weapon against creatures with highly developed olfactory senses—like dragons. When exposed to the noxious fumes, a dragon's sense of smell is rendered completely ineffective.

Out of stock. Pick up more at any magical fireworks stand.

SUNSTONE

This white stone is usually found atop a hill, where it is exposed to sunlight. It then becomes the source of luminance for its sister stones. The soft light emitted by such stones can brighten dark spaces far from any natural lighting.

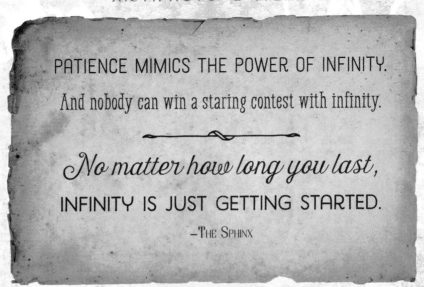

PATIENCE MIMICS THE POWER OF INFINITY.

And nobody can win a staring contest with infinity.

No matter how long you last,

INFINITY IS JUST GETTING STARTED.

—The Sphinx

TENTS *Tents are stored behind the barn.*

These often colorful, unfurnished, roomy shelters come in various sizes and have a steep, curving roof that slopes up to a high central pole. Atop each is a banner. One may enter through a front flap, which can be propped on rods to form a good-sized awning. The tents are closed to the outside world with a zipper. The best part of these Fablehaven tents is that their canvas walls are magically soundproof.

THIEF'S NET

A magical device for apprehending would-be robbers, these nets are kept in a magical box. If anyone opens the box without first deactivating the trap, the net springs out and wraps them up tightly.

TRANSDIMENSIONAL TRANSPORTERS

Unique transporters, these items are used in pairs for traveling instantly from one place to another. Both the tubs and the tin cans share a transdimensional space. If a person enters one of the tubs, he actually occupies both tubs at the same time, even though the two tubs are in different locations. The only catch is that the person can't get out of the second, destination tub himself—someone has to be near the tub to pull him out or he remains in the first tub. The tin cans work the same way and can be used to transport small objects.

Tub in secret attic is connected to Brazilian preserve.

A box of umite markers is in the caretaker's office, bottom drawer.

UMITE WAX

This wax is made by umites, a variety of sprites, who live in hive-like communities in the rainforests of the world. The wax is used to make magical candles and markers. When properly enchanted, these items can be used to send and receive sensitive messages and to secretly mark trails. A message written in umite wax is invisible to the eye until illuminated by the flame of a umite candle; the message is impossible to erase.

Property of Seth Sorenson. Well, sort of. I have to return it to the Singing Sisters.

VASILIS

One of the most fabled of the six great swords from a past age of wonder, Vasilis is also known as the Sword of Light and Darkness and is located behind the Totem Wall. The sword feels like an extension of the body instead of a weapon in the hand.

Vasilis reflects the heart of the one who wields it, and it magnifies the wielder's emotions. For example, one's courage could be greatly multiplied, and one's sense of purpose could become more clear.

WHITE MESH

This magical fabric is eight feet in diameter and is used to catch elusive creatures like the drumant, a tarantula-like arachnid that is virtually impossible to snag because it simply vanishes into thin air. When thrown over such a creature, the fabric reveals a lump and entangles the would-be escapee in the fabric. (*See also* Drumant.)

Do not try to use this to capture a fairy. Seriously. Do NOT try it. - Seth

WE HUMANS ARE CONFLICTED BEINGS.

Our beliefs don't always harmonize with our instincts,
and our behavior doesn't always reflect our beliefs.

WE CONSTANTLY STRUGGLE
WITH RIGHT AND WRONG.

*We wage war between the person we are
and the person we hope to become.*

We have a lot of practice wrestling with ourselves.

As a result, compared to magical creatures, we humans
are much more able to suppress our natural inclinations
in order to deliberately choose our identities.

—GRANDPA SORENSON

*Glad I'm
a Satyr.
—Newel*

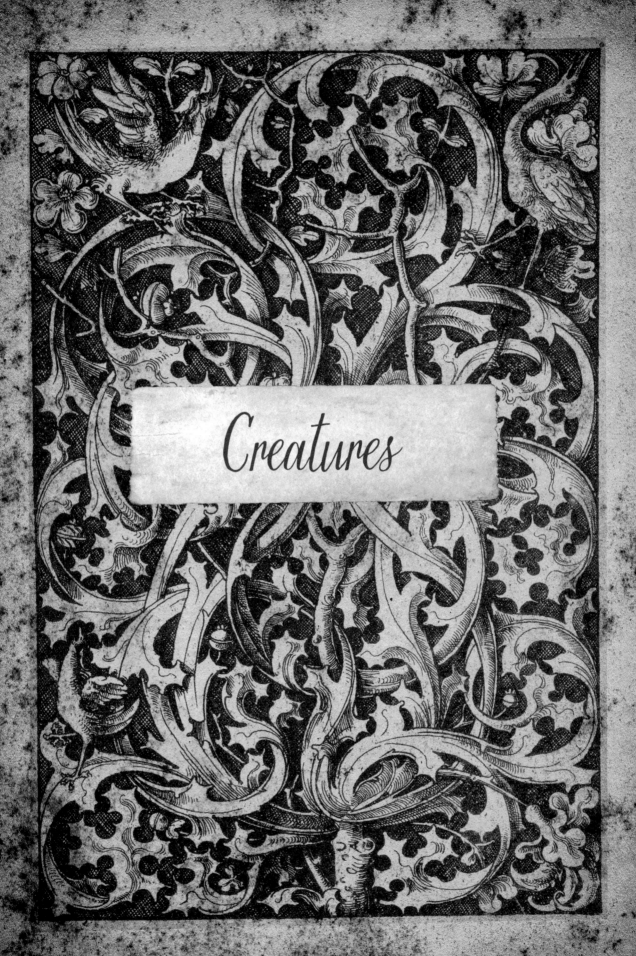

Creatures

Resides at Wyrmroost

ALCETAUR

Like a centaur but with the body of a moose. Extremely proficient with the bow. Less trustworthy than centaurs. Never more at home than when out in the wild.

APPARITION

A ghostly spirit that appears in human form. Contrary to some myths and legends, apparitions are often friendly and helpful beings sent to warn and provide aid.

ASTRID

These mysterious creatures look like large golden owls with human faces. Note: They once served as the elite guards to the Fairy King. Their gilded feathers have faint brown markings, and their faces have creamy, flawless complexions. They can communicate telepathically. There are only ninety-three astrids currently in existence.

Kendra kissed an astrid! Lots of them. ☺ *S.S.*

And Seth was turned into a giant mutant walrus! K.S.

BASILISK

Giant, snakelike monsters with dragonlike scales, basilisks inhabit Wyrmroost and the dragon sanctuaries and are extremely dangerous. Mere eye contact with a basilisk means death. Their breath is also fatal, and their skin exudes a deadly poison that is transferred through any weapon that pierces it.

BLIX

Vampiric in nature, blixes connect with their victims through a bite. Three standard varieties of blixes are lectoblixes, narcoblixes, and viviblixes. The lectoblix remains young by draining its victims of their youth. It looks much like any human being, although without its life-sustaining nourishment, the lectoblix ages quickly.

The narcoblix is capable of exerting control over its victims while they sleep, and the viviblix can temporarily reanimate the dead.

None of these creatures are good. Not the way we think of good. None are safe. Much of morality is peculiar to mortality. The best creatures here are merely not evil.

—Grandpa Sorenson

Brownies once made me brownies. K.S.

BROWNIE

Brownies are the only magical creatures at Fablehaven with permission to enter the caretaker's residence at will. The portals through which they pass into human homes are guarded by magic, preventing other creatures of the forest from using them. Brownies are remarkable craftsmen who love to make and repair all sorts of things and who accept no compensation for their services. They seldom talk to strangers, and they don't take requests, but if one leaves a project ready for them, they will see it done. Their motto is "We all do what we do." (*See also* Brownie Hole; Nipsy.)

And they are excellent bakers! Leave a few ingredients on the counter overnight and see what they come up with!

Watch out if these guys go dark! S.S.

Centaurs are jerks! S.S.

CENTAUR

Brilliant thinkers, gifted artisans, and formidable warriors, these muscular creatures have a human head and torso fused to a horse's body. Centaurs tend to be self-important and often look down on others, in particular, satyrs. They neither seek nor appreciate admiration from lesser creatures and fiercely protect their own property.

They currently reside at Grunhold, under the leadership of Graymane. Though generally aloof, they have forged alliances with caretakers in times of emergency.

CHIMERA

These frightening creatures inhabit Living Mirage. Chimeras have the head of a lion, the body of a goat, and the tail of a venomous snake. Thronis, the sky giant, possesses a jade chimera figurine that, when enchanted, becomes a formidable, living weapon in the hands of its master. (*See also* Precious Figurines.)

CYCLOPS

A species of giant twice the height of a man, the Cyclops is a one-eyed giant who usually wields a club or cudgel.

MESOPOTAMIAN TRICLOPS

The Mesopotamian Triclops has three eye sockets arranged like the points of a triangle and a skull that tapers to a blunt point. They are highly resistant to magic and have been known to glimpse the future.

DRUMANT

A drumant looks like a tarantula with a tail and is extremely dangerous because of its aggressive nature and deadly poisonous bite. A drumant can warp light to distort its location, making it virtually impossible to detect. Use the magical white mesh fabric to reveal its location and entangle it when it attempts to flee. Drumants may be kept at bay by sprinkling sawdust and garlic. (*See also* White Mesh.)

DWARF

Waist-high, stocky men and women who wear homespun clothing, these creatures live underground at Fablehaven and prefer to keep to themselves. It's sometimes tricky to distinguish between male and female dwarves because women dwarves have whiskers and are known for their unladylike manners.

We believe there is a magical dwarf among the colony at Fablehaven. His identity and intentions remain questionable.

ZOGO

A stocky little dwarf who belongs to Thronis, the Sky Giant, at Wyrmroost. He commands a pride of griffins. He carries a short sword and a battered shield emblazoned with a yellow fist and wears a dented iron helmet over his head—all indicative of his experience in battle. His bronzed skin, black eyes, and stubbly beard add to his hardy appearance.

And his megaphone is annoying! S.S.

THE ETERNALS

Five Eternals are linked to each of the five ancient artifacts, or keys to Zzyzx. In exchange for virtual immortality, these once ordinary men and/or women volunteered to be part of the lock that holds Zzyzx closed and are the final obstacles in gaining admittance to the prison. The artifacts can't be used to open the prison until all five Eternals are dead. Nobody knows their identities or locations.

▷ I Know! S.S.

FAIRY

Beautiful, magical winged creatures, fairies can appear as hummingbirds, bumblebees, butterflies, or dragonflies to the mortal eye. In their true form, fairies gleam more brilliantly than any flower, much like how the sun outshines the moon. They range in size from one to four inches, but when enchanted, their lithe, athletic bodies can become human sized.

Some fairies look Asian, African, or European, while some are otherworldly with blue skin and emerald-green hair. Popular hair colors include platinum silver, fiery red, honey blonde, and midnight black. Their wings are typically their most stunning feature. Most wings are patterned after butter-flies or dragonflies but are more elegantly shaped and radiantly colored. Some even look like stained glass.

Fairies are aware of their beauty and love to gaze at their reflections. They consider looking at themselves such a delight that at times they will deny the pleasure to others. They tend to be vain, selfish creatures with little empathy. Fairies rarely use Silvian, their language, except to trade insults. They pre-tend not to care what mortals think of them, but if given a compliment, they will blush with delight and seek for another. Flattery is one of the best means of capturing them.

Fairies are master gardeners and have a knack for mak-ing vegetation bloom. A good number are kept in captivity, but many more still live in the wild. A captive fairy becomes

If you do capture one, do NOT, I repeat, DO NOT keep the fairy indoors overnight. -Seth

obedient and submissive and cannot use magic to escape. Fairies are highly territorial, nonmigratory creatures and will happily make their home in a place where food, gardens, and other enchanted creatures are plentiful. Supernatural laws dictate, however, that if caught and kept indoors too long, a fairy becomes an imp. (See also Imp.)   *See. Told you.*

Fairies of all types can be found on the magical preserves. Downy Fountain Sprites hale from the island of Roti—their bodies are coated with a pale blue fuzz. Albino Nightgrifters are milky white fairies from Borneo with moth-like wings speckled with flecks of black. The tiny Banda Sea Sunwings are not even an inch tall, with vibrant butterfly wings that resemble stained glass. Some Arizona fairies come in earthy shades.

There are fairies with thorny wings and tails, fairies covered in reptilian scales with chameleonic abilities to match different backgrounds, fairies with plumage that fans out from their heads and bodies, fairies with tiger-striped wings, fairies that look like glowing June bugs, and fairies with bat-like wings.

Fairies may seem innocuous, but their magic can transform ordinary objects into weapons—thorns may become spears, snail shells shields, and flower petals battle-axes. They also can blast steam from the ends of wands and turn bubbles into anything from balls of fire to miniature globes of ice. Fairies have been known to shatter glass, turn creatures to stone or other misshapen forms, and heal injuries.

Been there, done that. S.S.

FAIRY QUEEN

There are no words to adequately describe the Fairy Queen. Tall and graceful, she shines with ethereal beauty. Widely considered the most powerful figure in all of fairydom, she is not of this world and her habitation is untouched by darkness. Her beneficent influence is best perceived at the Fairy Shrines. The shrine at Fablehaven is located on the island in the Naiads' Pond. Through the eyes of her sister fairies she can see all the spheres they inhabit, and on occasion she can speak in their minds.

Becoming Fairykind

Becoming fairykind means that the Fairy Queen and her fairies have infused a person with their magic. Ordinarily, a mortal must drink magical milk to perceive magic, and the effects wear off after a night asleep. After becoming fairykind, or a handmaiden of the Fairy Queen, a person will exhibit these magical properties indefinitely.

Once fairykind, a person is immune to distracter spells, can understand the Silvian language and others related to it, can see in the dark, and becomes resistant to mind control. A portion of the magical energy that naturally dwells in fairies now dwells in the person, and he or she can recharge magical objects and transfer some of that energy to fairies. This person can also command fairies in the name of the queen to offer help or divulge information.

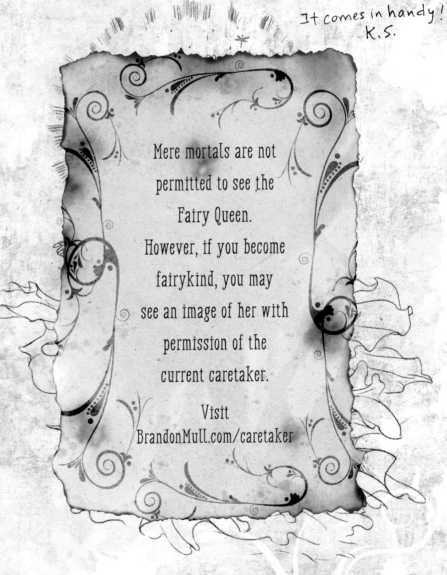

It comes in handy!
K.S.

Mere mortals are not permitted to see the Fairy Queen. However, if you become fairykind, you may see an image of her with permission of the current caretaker.

Visit
BrandonMull.com/caretaker

JINN HARP FAIRY

So beautiful!
K.S.

Only two Jinn Harp fairies are known to exist. They are among the most notable and regal fairies with wings like shimmering veils of gold and elegant feathers that stream behind them like ribbons of light. They are known for their mesmerizing songs, which can be sweet, hopeful, longing, and heartbreaking all at once.

One Jinn Harp fairy was tracked down near Mongolia. The other is said to have her own shrine in a Tibetan sanctuary.

NIPSY

Bring a magnifying glass!
S.S.

These tiny creatures are the smallest of the fairy folk. They are related to brownies but are only a fraction of their height. Like brownies, they are master artisans but instead of mending, salvaging, and recycling, nipsies tend to create from scratch, using natural resources to

acquire their raw materials. They are fascinated by shiny metal and stones and have a knack for finding them. Though they cast no magic spells and are not known as being aggressive, they are adept at preparing traps and planting venomous, carnivorous vegetation. (*See also* Brownie; Seven Kingdoms of the Nipsies.)

PIXIE

A pixie is a type of fairy. Among the most notable are the Norwegian pixies because of their magical cocoons that offer protection from cold winters and from would-be predators. This pixie loses its wings in the winter and spends the coldest months inside the small green pod. It emerges in the spring with a beautiful set of wings. (*See also* Pixie Cocoon.)

FIREDRAKE

These small, fire-breathing creatures have long white fangs, green eyes, and are lightning fast. They inhabit the dragon sanctuary at Wyrmroost.

GARGOYLE

These large, winged monsters have razor-sharp claws, horns of various shapes and sizes, and are formidable foes in combat.

GIANT

Enormous, strong creatures, giants have insatiable appetites and can get worked into a frenzy when they smell or see blood. The different races of giants embody a variety of attributes.

Kendra's next boyfriend! S.S.

FOG GIANT

The fog giant, though slow and clumsy, is also a
bloodthirsty, vicious killer. Inhabiting the marshes
of Fablehaven, they are primitive creatures who
wear tattered, matted furs. Their filthy bodies
are smeared with oily muck, and their skin is a
sickly bluish-gray color. Their hair and beards
are typically long and tangled with slime. Fog
giants sense prey by smell and hearing.

STEPPE GIANT

These burly armored nomads are half the height of a tree and are found at Living
Mirage. These ornery giants will get into a brawl without provocation. In ancient
times, groups of a dozen or fewer were known to sack entire cities.

THRONIS

An ancient and clever giant, Thronis is a sky giant and several times larger than a fog
giant. He lives atop Stormcrag at Wyrmroost and is a gifted sorcerer. In addition to his
brute strength, he demonstrates mental prowess and can temper the climate through the
use of a dark orb. A white orb allows him to gaze over almost all of Wyrmroost and
even beyond the walls without leaving his fortress.

He looks like an ordinary man except for his size. His wide mouth, longish nose,
salt-and-pepper eyebrows, and gently sagging body give him the appearance of being
in his mid-sixties. He wears a white toga and has an enchanted silver collar around
his neck, which forces him to always be truthful. His native tongue is Jiganti, but he
speaks English fluently, along with several other languages.

If I ever run into Thronis again,
I'll give him a pie. He loves meat pies!
P.S. But let's hope we never have to meet
again. He might prefer human pies.
—Seth

GIANT WALRUS

Like the milch cow, the giant walrus is revered by all fairydom and is one of the
oldest animals on the planet. Located in Greenland, the giant walrus is valued for
her magical properties and produces a butter much like Viola the milch cow's milk.
(*See also* Milch Cow; Potions.)

GOBLIN

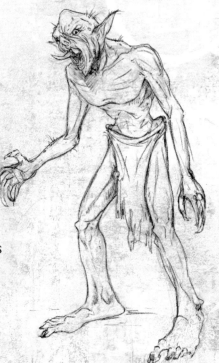

These fearsome, vicious creatures differ in appearance, but all are grotesquely hideous. Some goblins have slitted yellow eyes, puckered noses, balding heads fringed with webby hair, and faces that look like dried, shriveled cantaloupes. Others have knobby heads, shriveled noses, and tusks. Often their ribs, collarbones, and pelvises jut out hideously, and their gangly, sinuous arms routinely end in leathery fingers with hooked claws. Their skin is sometimes maroon and crisscrossed with spidery networks of bulging veins, but can also be pink and orange and marred by scars.

SLAGGO AND VOORSH

Both short, bony, and greenish, with beady eyes and batwing ears, these two goblins have managed the Fablehaven dungeon for centuries. They are scrawny, servile creatures who live to carry out orders from their superiors. They enjoy dwelling in the darkness, supervising their dismal domain.

GOLEM

True golems were once actual, living creatures made of stone, mud, or sand, but they've long since passed out of human knowledge. Manufactured golem, also of stone, mud, or sand, were fashioned after the original golem but are mindless puppets who exist only to obey orders.

DULLION

These gigantic humanoid figures are pseudo-golems fashioned of straw, tar, or other materials and animated by a powerful spell. Easier to create than golems, dullions usually have short legs with large feet, massive torsos, long arms, and oversized heads with gaping mouths but no eyes. A dullion can exert an incredible amount of force but cannot act under its own will.

HUGO

The only known true golem is Hugo. He was originally a manufactured golem, but a powerful enchantment granted him a semblance of life. Over nine feet tall, Hugo is broad-chested and has thick limbs and disproportionately large hands and feet. He has an oblong head with a square jaw and a crude nose, mouth, and ears. His eyes are a pair of vacant hollows that sit beneath a jutting brow. He is useful for tasks that involve heavy labor. Gifted with a rudimentary intelligence, he has developed a will of his own but still obeys commands if he can understand them. Sometimes, those issuing the command must demonstrate physically what they wish him to do.

Maybe the best thing about Fablehaven! S.S.

Hey!?! — Newel

PLEASE DO NOT OBSESS OVER

CHOICES YOU CANNOT CHANGE.

MISTAKES HAPPEN.

LEARN FROM THE PAST, BUT

CONCENTRATE ON THE

PRESENT AND THE FUTURE.

—Patton

GRIFFIN

This large, winged creature has the head, torso, and talons of an eagle but the body and rear legs of a lion. Its long, hooked beak is made for tearing its prey apart. Its shiny golden-brown feathers carry it aloft as it nimbly takes to the sky. Griffins can handle harsh weather better than dragons.

Flying
in their
talons
feels like
Hang
gliding!
S. S.

HARPY

Found at Living Mirage, these long-haired, wiry women have wings instead of arms, talons instead of legs, and sharp, pointed teeth. A scratch from their poisonous talons leaves a victim with a painful, deep, yellow-edged, lethal wound. Victim will die within minutes if not treated. The best chance of surviving harpy poison is to use a unicorn horn.

HAWKBEAR

I'm glad I've never seen one of these up close!
K. S.

Built like a bear, this creature has the shaggy fur of a yak, a thick, hawk-like beak, and a hairless tail with a bulbous knob at the end. It stands twice the height of a grizzly bear, emits a sound halfway between a screech and a roar, and is known to inhabit the terrain below Stormcrag. None appear to have been admitted to Fablehaven.

HYDRA

A hydra has a bulky body and no fewer than eight heads at the end of as many serpentine necks. The draconic heads are roughly the size of coffins, but the heads differ slightly in size and appearance. There is always one head that governs the others. In order to defeat a hydra, one should confuse and distract the other heads and then attack the governing head.

Be warned: every time a head is severed, two new ones will grow in its place.

IMP

A fairy trapped indoors from sunset to sunrise will change into an imp. Imps come in just as many shapes and sizes as fairies. They normally stand only a few inches high, but can be magically grown to over six feet tall. Some have crooked backs, some have humps, some have horns or antlers, and some have bulging cysts or tails. They have weathered, leathery skin, and nubs instead of wings. Imps can appear as rats or tarantulas to the mortal eye.

Unlike the narcissistic fairies, imps despise themselves. Just as fairies are drawn to beauty, imps surround themselves with ugliness. Their personalities remain similar. They are still shallow and self-absorbed, but they are more spiteful and jealous and miserable.

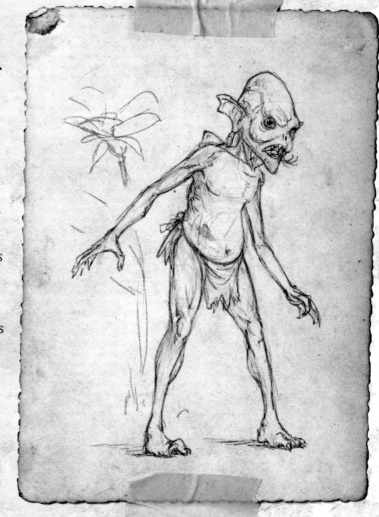

JACKALOPE

This creature, found on the Lost Mesa preserve, is a large rabbit with a short pair of forked antlers. Jackalopes are said to bring good luck.

There is a jinn held captive in a specialized dungeon cell at Fablehaven.

JINN

Jinn are the entities through which the myth of genies arose. They are powerful but oftentimes evil. One may negotiate with an imprisoned jinn for a favor, but jinns are extremely cunning, so take great care.

Negotiations with a jinn require an extreme level of vulnerability and honesty. The jinn may ask any three questions, which must be answered with absolute truthfulness.

If all three questions are answered honestly, the jinn grants a favor.

If the petitioner lies, the jinn is set free and gains power over the petitioner.

If the petitioner fails to answer a question, the jinn remains captive but may exact a penalty.

The one question a jinn is not permitted to ask is a person's given name because knowing his or her name automatically gives the jinn power over that person.

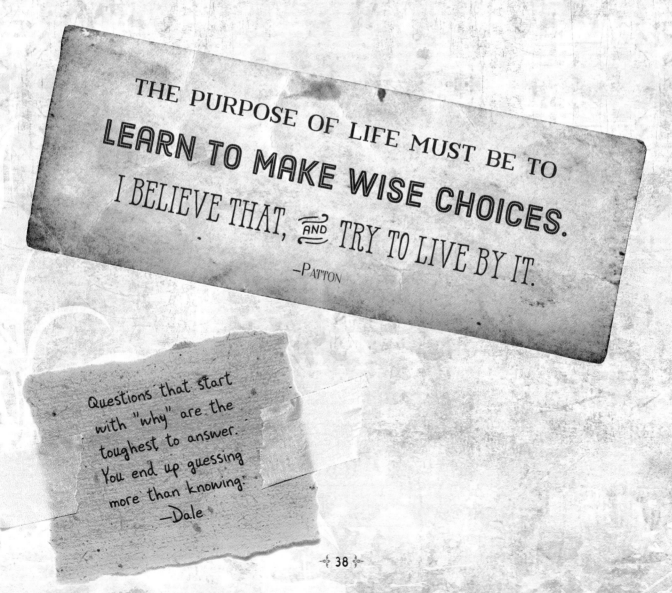

THE PURPOSE OF LIFE MUST BE TO LEARN TO MAKE WISE CHOICES. I BELIEVE THAT, AND TRY TO LIVE BY IT.

—PATTON

Questions that start with "why" are the toughest to answer. You end up guessing more than knowing.
—Dale

KACHINA

Nature spirits worshipped by the Native Americans at the Lost Mesa preserve, kachinas are extremely territorial and will kill trespassers. Some Native Americans impersonate kachina by wearing elaborate masks. Many of the real kachinas appear as humanoid coyotes, hawks, bobcats, scorpions, and other beasts.

I've seen enough of these to last a lifetime. K.S.

KARKADANN

A creature of Living Mirage, the karkadann is a formidable animal resembling a rhinoceros with one sentient horn. It is known for its fearsome roar and its speed in charging opponents.

KOBOLD

Relatives of goblins, these evil creatures can appear deceptively handsome to nonmagical onlookers. Only someone who can see past their enchantment knows they are hideously disfigured creatures with bald, scabrous heads, eyes that are little more than puckered slits, noses that are malformed cavities, and lipless, toothless, crusty mouths with blackened tongues. Their bodies are often covered with pus-filled sores, their lumpy fingers bulge with warts, and their voices tend to be pinched and gravelly.

LAMMASU

Servants of light, these proud creatures resemble bulls with the heads of men. One resides at Living Mirage, guarding the secret entrance to the dungeons. Although he is not an evil being, he is bound by covenant to slay any who attempt to escape the dungeons.

LEPRECHAUN

These magical little men pad their coffers by finding and taking lost and hidden treasures. They can't resist unattended gold and have pockets that can hold indefinite amounts of it. When they are caught, their magic is useless. The best way to dupe them is with either gold or whiskey, for both cloud their judgment.

CORMAC

This miniature miser lives at Fablehaven. He has a bristly auburn beard, a knobby nose, and speaks with an Irish brogue. He wears a red frock coat and an outdated hat. He can be caught, but never with the same trap twice. (*See also Lady Luck.*)

LICH

An undead creature, the Fablehaven lich resides in the Grim Marsh. More intelligent than a zombie, a lich appears desiccated or completely skeletal. The Fablehaven lich has the ability to control lesser undead creatures and use them as servant soldiers. For this reason, zombies should NEVER be admitted to Fablehaven.

LIMBERJACK

A featureless, primitive puppet about nine inches high and made entirely of dark wood. Its wrists, elbows, shoulders, neck, ankles, knees, hips, waist, and knuckles are connected by golden hooks. When enchanted by Muriel the witch, her limberjack became enlarged and gained the ability to dance on its own.

Still looking for a way to reanimate the limberjack Mendigo.

Never thought I'd miss him. S.S.

LYCANTHROPE

A fierce wolfish creature the size of a bear. Commonly termed "werewolf," it has the ability to turn into a man. It has been spotted at Fablehaven at least twice during Midsummer's Eve.

Unclear if this creature still resides at Fablehaven. When Graulas destroyed the treaty, it is possible the lycanthrope left the preserve.

CHOICES DETERMINE *character.*

—GRAULAS

MAGICAL PLANTS

CHOKEPOD

Dodging these is NOT a fun party game! K.S.

Ranging in size from a softball to a beach ball, these toxic floating bulbs are brown and black and almost spherical, with tops that are somewhat pinched. When touched, these fibrous balls burst and release a lethal gas that travels through the respiratory system or is absorbed through the skin. The toxins gradually liquefy the body until even the remains vaporize into fumes that are absorbed by other chokepods. Anyone in the vicinity of a ruptured pod is sure to suffer death.

LOTUS BLOSSOM

Even a tiny nibble of this blossom transports a person into a lethargic trance filled with vivid hallucinations. These plants have an intoxicating smell, a divine taste, and are more addictive than most drugs. Sampling a lotus blossom awakens a craving that can never be satisfied. Many people have wasted their lives pursuing and consuming these bewitching flowers.

No matter how careful you are, there is always the chance of running across something more terrible than you are prepared to handle.

—Coulter

STINGBULB

Nearly extinct, this magical fruit is actually a living entity with the power to clone a person. A sting-bulb tree produces just a few pieces of fruit per year. This fruit must be used within a narrow window of time or it becomes useless.

After stinging a subject, the bulb will grow slowly and look like a large purple yam. Next, there will be a crunching, crack-ing sound, and part of the clone will break through the purplish husk. Before long, the entire clone emerges as an exact replica of the original, even down to the clothing.

It takes about ninety minutes for the metamorphosis to occur, and the clone only survives for three or four days. While it is animated, it retains most of the memories of its host but has its own consciousness. Stingbulb clones are single-mindedly loyal and will obey the commands given them after they are created.

A stingbulb can often be found in the front pocket of the knapsack. Use it wisely!

MANTICORE

This creature has a lion's body with a man's head and a scorpion's tail. It resides at Living Mirage.

MILCH COW

A milch cow is a colossal, magical bovine whose milk, blood, dung, sweat, tears, and saliva have different magical properties. Her manure is the finest fertilizer in the world, coaxing plants to mature much more quickly than usual and sometimes to reach incredible proportions. Farmers using milch cow fertilizer can reap multiple harvests from a field in a single season.

The milk of a milch cow is the preferred drink of fairykind, and the breed is nourished and worshipped by all creatures of fairydom. They place daily enchantments on her food and make secret offerings to honor and strengthen her. Mortals who drink the milk of a milch cow can see the true nature of magical creatures.

Drink the milk! K.S.

Each magical preserve has a creature like a milch cow that supplies magical produce for the fairies in those lands. These magical animals look like their counterparts but are gargantuan in size. (*See also* Giant Walrus; Potions.)

VIOLA

Born on a preserve in the Pyrenees Mountains, Viola was around one hundred years old when she was brought to America by ship. At that time she was already larger than an elephant and has been gaining size each year, although her growth has slowed over the last few years.

Currently between forty and fifty feet tall, she fills the entire barn at Fablehaven. Her hooves are the size of hot tubs, her teats the size of punching bags. Her mooing sounds like a foghorn.

MINOTAUR

Fablehaven is home to approximately two dozen minotaurs. Part man, part bull, these beasts stand a head taller than most men and come in various shades of fur, from chestnut brown to black. They have wide horns, a bulky musculature, and reek like livestock. The minotaur has an acute sense of smell. It is extremely strong and prefers heavy weapons such as the mace and battle-axe. These hefty weapons can slow down a minotaur, giving quick opponents an advantage.

NYMPH

Minor deities of field and stream, nymphs typically shy away from mortals and are often wooed by satyrs. Some nymphs have been known to choose a mortal life to pursue a mortal love.

DRYAD

These tall, graceful wood nymphs weave leaves and twigs throughout their long tresses and wear flowing robes that look like foliage. Some have fair skin, some bronzed.

Best page. —Newel

They are the guardians of the Fairy Shrine at Stony Vale Preserve.

HAMADRYAD

These youthful wood nymphs are more spirited and flirtatious than their dryad cousins and can often be found socializing with the satyrs among the pavilions. Hamadryads are also beings of the forest, but each hamadryad's life is inextricably linked to a particular tree. When the tree dies, the hamadryad dies with it unless the connection is passed through a seed from the original tree to a new one. Because their trees can be reborn as seedlings, hamadryads can be virtually immortal.

THE LEGEND OF EPHIRA IS BOTH SAD AND HAUNTING. HER BEAUTY WAS INTOXICATING. HER LUST FOR REVENGE: ALL-CONSUMING. —P.B.

NAIAD

These ancient water nymphs are protectors of the Fairy Queen's Island Shrine at Fablehaven. They beckon unsuspecting travelers to the water, only to pull them in and drown them. Since the comparatively short lifespan of humans is viewed as ridiculous, naiads find killing mortals absurd and funny, no more tragic than squashing a moth. Naiads are always looking for ways to amuse themselves. Not immortal in the true sense of the word, they may live indefinitely as long as they remain in the water. Time is irrelevant to them because they live in the moment, never dwelling on the future or the past. (*See also* The Hidden Pond.)

For time and eternity, I shall forever love my Lena.
—P.B.

OGRESS

As homely and ornery as her male counterpart, the ogress at Fablehaven has a broad, flat face with saggy earlobes that hang almost to her hefty shoulders. She has a misshapen bosom, a bulky body, rough, avocado-green skin, and graying, shaggy, matted hair. Nearly blind, she uses her sense of smell to detect prey. Despite her cumbersome size and lack of physical endurance, she is surprisingly fast. She resides in a hill in a lair that has a stone chimney that looks like a well. At the base of the chimney she regularly cooks a delicious meat and vegetable stew.

Newell and Doren are going to be stew meat if they keep messing with her. Ruth S.

She has to catch me first! —Newel

I don't view most magical creatures as good or evil. WHAT THEY ARE LARGELY GOVERNS HOW THEY ACT. In order to be good, you must recognize the difference between right and wrong and strive to choose the right.

TO BE TRULY EVIL YOU MUST DO THE CONTRARY. *Being good or evil is a choice.*

—GRANDPA SORENSON

PERYTON

This large, winged stag has a massive rack of deadly black antlers, golden fur, and feathered wings and hindquarters. Its razor-sharp yellow teeth drip with foam when a peryton is agitated, and the creature emits an ear-splitting, thunderous roar. Its hooves are also dangerously sharp. Despite its wings, the peryton is limited to how long it may remain airborne. Instead of actually flying, perytons travel in a series of long, wing-assisted leaps.

There is a large herd at Wyrmroost. Not recommended for Fablehaven.

Warren did not want to be killed by a deer.
S. S.

PHANTOM

These malevolent apparitions are known to haunt the Hall of Dread. It is fatal to gaze into their eyes. If imprisoned, most phantoms will beg and cajole and offer servitude in exchange for their freedom.

PHOENIX

This powerful bird resides in the dragon sanctuary at Wyrmroost. Its magical feathers, which can be made into arrows, are one of only three standard items that can kill immortal beings. The other two are dragon's breath and a unicorn's horn.

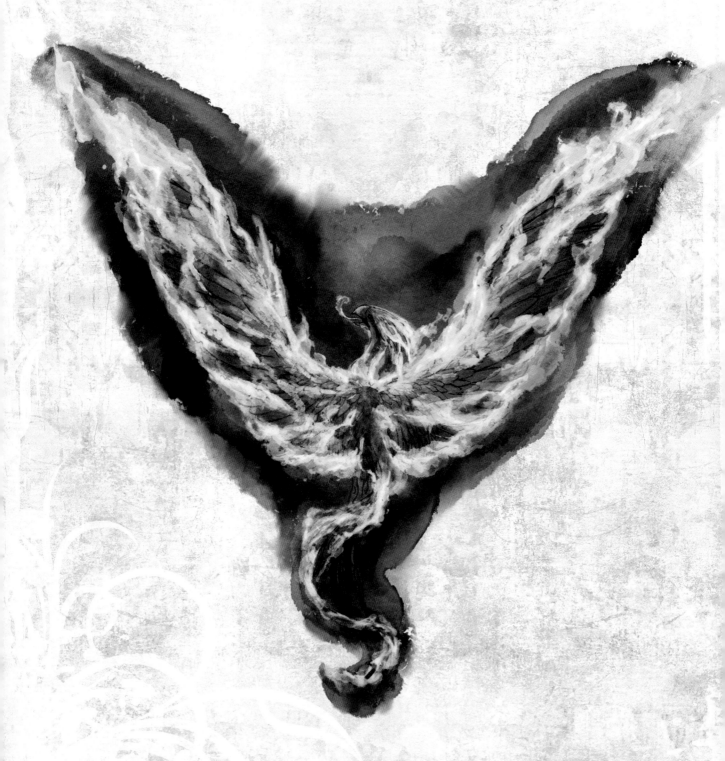

REVENANT

Revenants are undead creatures with sickly, leprous skin, open sores, and blotchy discolorations. One protects the entrance to the hidden artifact at Fablehaven. A revenant is able to instill an irrational, suffocating terror in its victims that manifests physically as well as mentally. After contact with a revenant, a person's skin is bleached white and the body paralyzed, leaving the victim unable to speak or move, and barely able to think. Ultimately, this fear can kill a person.

Lodged in the neck of the revenant at Fablehaven is a nail strong in dark magic. Without it, the revenant is not very formidable; with it, he becomes one of the most intimidating and dangerous creatures in existence. Care must be taken with this item, however, for if the nail comes in contact with the skin, its dark power takes possession of that person.

Nothing a pair of pliers can't solve. S.S. P.S. I have a cool idea for a video game called "Revenant Wars."

ROC

A roc nesting area is within fifteen minutes of the great ziggurat at Living Mirage. Be watchful!

Also known as a simurgh, this enormous bird is the size of a plane, with talons large enough to crush a school bus. It has an earsplitting cry and preys on elephants and aurochs in order to feed its brood. It prefers light to darkness.

SATYR

Half goat, half man, these creatures are known to be ill-mannered, frivolous, and lazy. The most surefire way to scare a satyr away is to mention work. They possess boundless energy, are quick and nimble, and enjoy spending their time dancing, wrestling, and playing games. From the waist up, their human forms are mostly naked, but some wear vests. Satyrs have pointy horns just above their foreheads. The fur on their bodies ranges in color from various browns, reds, and grays to whites, golds, and black.

NEWEL AND DOREN

The most notable satyrs at Fablehaven, Newel and Doren are best friends. Newel's fur is slightly redder than Doren's, and he has longer horns. They own a portable TV and love to idle away their time watching it and playing tennis. They also like to barter items such as gold and alcohol for batteries. The two have been permitted free access to the yard but not the house.

The real heroes of Fablehaven! -Newel

Do not trade batteries for gold. We don't want to introduce modern technology to Fablehaven any more than neccesary. That means you, Seth.

SHADOW CHARMER

A shadow charmer enjoys brotherhood with the creatures of the night. His emotions cannot be manipulated, and nothing escapes his gaze. He hears and comprehends the secret languages of darkness. A shadow charmer can shade walk—away from bright light, he will be nearly invisible. When in the shade, even vigilant eyes will pass over the shadow charmer, particularly if he holds still.

Although no two shadow charmers are exactly alike, each has certain talents that emerge over time: some can project fear, some can lower the temperature in a room, some can quench flames. All possess an unusual connection with the undead. They are also immune to the chilling influence of phantoms and wraiths.

Seth was here!

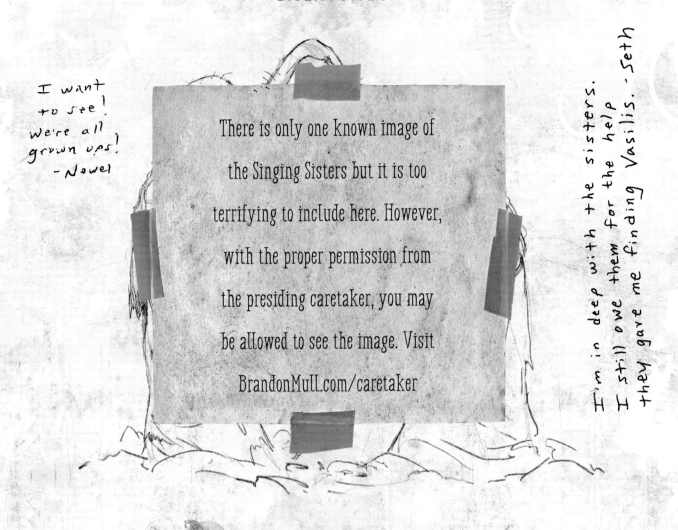

There is only one known image of the Singing Sisters but it is too terrifying to include here. However, with the proper permission from the presiding caretaker, you may be allowed to see the image. Visit BrandonMull.com/caretaker

I want to see! We're all grown ups! —Newel

I'm in deep with the sisters. I still owe them for the help they gave me finding Vasilis. —Seth

SINGING SISTERS

The Singing Sisters dwell on an island in the Mississippi River and are protected by a gentle distracter spell. One who desires to bargain with thewm must seek them out in their island lair, where a number of trolls run around at their beck and call. One may bargain with Wilna, Orna, and Berna for access to their oracular powers, but their assistance comes at a steep price—if one bargains and loses, he forfeits his life.

In their damp and slimy home, the sisters stand, handless, their wrists fused together in such a way that forces them to stand in a circle. They are surrounded by several puddles, each home to a giant maggot. When asked for guidance, the sisters begin to sing in unison, the puddles glow, and the maggots burst to release an inky cloud of deep purple. Within this cloud, the visitor is shown what he or she desires.

There is great power in harboring a single goal.
—THE SPHINX

THE SENTINEL

Anyone wishing to approach the Singing Sisters must first stop at the shack outside their domain. There, travelers are greeted by the sentinel, an old man with a carved walking stick, the white stubble around the sides of his head his only hair. To see the sisters, visitors must convince the sentinel that they have a valid purpose.

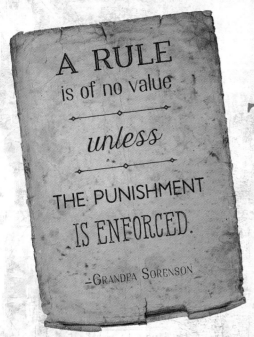

A RULE
is of no value
unless
THE PUNISHMENT
IS ENFORCED.

—GRANDPA SORENSON

SIRRUSH

These vicious, scaly flying dogs travel in packs. They currently inhabit Living Mirage.

SKINWALKER

Skinwalkers are humans able to transform themselves into an animal at will.

For more information, ask Neil from Lost Mesa.

Guardian of the Fairy Queen's Shrine at Living Mirage
Not to be confused with the shifty guy who himself the Sphinx. —Kendra

SPHINX

This creature has the body of a golden lion and the head of a woman. She has large, almond-shaped eyes the color of jade. Her sultry voice is not only audible to the ears but directly and powerfully penetrates the mind. Those wishing to pass this guardian must solve the riddles she presents them.

SWAMP HAG

Normally one is safe in Fablehaven if he or she stays on the marked paths, but this devious denizen of the swamp creates false paths that lead the unwary to their doom. (*See also* Great Marsh of Fablehaven.)

Pretty much the opposite of a nymph
—Newel

THYLACINE

Also known as Tasmanian tigers, thylacines look like large, striped greyhounds with long tails. Some of these magical creatures are gifted with the power of speech.

Many thylacines reside at Obsidian Waste,

but they're extinct elsewhere.

THE TOTEM WALL

Located in Canada, the Totem Wall serves an oracular purpose similar to the Singing Sisters.

Weatherworn and timeworn, this superbly crafted wooden structure spans an entire ravine and is made up of hundreds of animal faces: bears, wolves, deer, moose, elk, lynxes, beavers, otters, seals, walruses, eagles, owls, and many others. A diverse array of human faces is also represented, some male, some female, some old, some young, some fair, some hideous. On these faces are myriad expressions, some friendly, some furious, some wise, others ridiculous, others crafty, others ill, others smug, others frightened, and others serene. One may communicate with the wall by standing atop the low stump in front of it and addressing the host of faces.

Cheat sheet! I got in by speaking with Anyu the Hunter, Tootega the Crone, Yuralria the Dancer, and Chu the Beaver. The Hunter dude seemed the most reasonable! But be prepared to pay a price for whatever knowledge is given. —Seth

TROLL

These nefarious beings can be violent and unpredictable. Diverse breeds of troll reside in various locations on the preserves. Trolls vary in size and shape, but they are generally unsavory and best avoided.

CLIFF TROLL

Miserly recluses, treasure hoarders, and cunning negotiators, cliff trolls thrill at besting their opponents. They typically live in barely accessible caves in the side of steep precipices.

NERO

Nero is Fablehaven's resident cliff troll. He has a deep, silky voice and is built like a man with reptilian features. A few bright yellow markings decorate his glossy black scales. The thickness of his muscular physique makes him appear much larger than he is. He has a snout rather than a nose, bulging eyes that never blink, webbed fingers, a long gray tongue, and a row of sharp spines that run from the center of his forehead to the small of his back. Extendable fins help him glide through the air like a flying squirrel. Two of Nero's greatest possessions are a large stash of treasure and a seeing stone.

I HAVE TO BELIEVE OUR WILLS ARE STRONGER THAN THE ALLURE OF SOME FRUIT. TO BE SLAIN BY A TROLL OR CHIMERA WOULD BE SAD. BUT TO DESTROY OURSELVES TO SCRATCH AN ITCH WOULD BE SO PATHETIC I REFUSE TO ACCEPT THE POSSIBILITY.
—BRACKEN.

He's a punk and will do anything the Demon Graulus tells him to do! —Seth

HERMIT TROLL

The hermit troll is the smallest of trolls and rarely stays in one place very long, setting up temporary lairs anywhere from a quiet attic to under a bridge to inside a barrel. They prefer isolation, make no allies, and practice no harmful magic. They are considered the vermin of trollkind, talented at worming into cramped spaces and hiding, but little else.

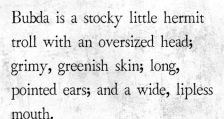

BUBDA

Bubda is a stocky little hermit troll with an oversized head; grimy, greenish skin; long, pointed ears; and a wide, lipless mouth.

MOUNTAIN TROLL

Along with a reputation for immense size and strength, mountain trolls are notorious for their stupidity. They love jokes and can often be won over by clever pranks.

UDNAR

Udnar the mountain troll resides at the heart of the (unsolvable) Tauran Maze in Grunold and is a smelly, enormous beast with thick, rhinoceros-like flesh and cruel spikes that protrude from his shoulders, forearms, thighs, and shins.

Bubda is awesome! No matter what he says, I'm way better than him at yahtzee!
— Seth

Nearly Unsolvable! - seth
P.S. udnar rules!

A community of river trolls lives along the left riverbank near the Beckoning grove.

RIVER TROLL

These scaly green monsters have oversized heads, wide mouths with thick lips, gaping nostrils, large ears, gill slits in their necks, and sinuous muscles. The northern river troll is afraid of the sun, while its eastern cousin is not as troubled by it. River trolls consider humans an extraordinary delicacy and, given the opportunity, will devour them with much ceremony.

UMITE

These little sprites live in hive-like communities in the rainforests of the world. Like bees, they make honey and wax. The wax is used to make magical candles and markers.

UNICORN

Guardians of the fairy world, unicorns are generally solitary creatures. They love deeply, but from a distance. They experience extraordinary clarity. They wander and heal and serve. However, these magnificent horses with pure white fur and gleaming horns are so rare that some believe they no longer exist. They are elusive creatures of extraordinary purity. Long ago, they were hunted to near extinction by wizards greedy for their horns.

A unicorn's translucent, pearly horn is its glory because it exhibits potent magical properties. During a unicorn's lifespan it grows three horns. It sheds the first two as it matures, sort of like humans losing baby teeth. The first horn of a unicorn is a powerful

object. It purifies whatever it touches, cures any sickness, neutralizes any poison, and eliminates any disease. This first horn can only be found or given away— it cannot be stolen. The object radiates such purity that even the most jaded scoundrels would be overwhelmed with enough guilt and remorse at the thought of stealing it to render them incapable of carrying out the robbery. Unicorns are capable of assuming human form, but if a unicorn loses its third horn, it will be trapped as a human.

Kendra's favorite page!
S.S.

Seth isn't always wrong...
K.S.

WHIRLIGIG

Fablehaven jargon for any magical animal of subhuman intelligence.

WHISPERHOUND

The whisperhound is not a living creature but rather an enchantment. When one brushes past an icy cold pocket in the dungeons, it is most likely a whisperhound. This unseen guardian becomes quite ferocious if a prisoner breaks out of a cell.

WITCH

Some mortal women choose the dark path of borrowing power from demons and eventually become witches. The most adept are capable of amazing magical feats. Though witches can be useful under certain circumstances, they must be approached with care and should never be trusted.

MURIEL TAGGERT

Once the intelligent, lovely wife of a previous caretaker of Fablehaven, Muriel became a frequent visitor to some of the darker portions of the forest, where she consorted with unsavory beings who tutored her. Before long, she became enamored with the power of witchcraft and fell under the influence of her dark tutors. She became unstable. Her husband tried to help her, but she was already too demented. When she tried to aid some of the foul denizens of the woods in a treacherous act of rebellion, her husband called in assistance and had her imprisoned in the shack, bound with a bristly rope with thirteen knots.

Though Muriel chews on the knots until her gums bleed, powerful magic holds them in place. She can loosen none on her own, though it doesn't seem to stop her from trying. Mortals can undo the knots by asking a favor and repeating the words "Of my own free will, I sever this knot" and then blowing on a knot. When a knot is released, the air begins to vibrate and the ground seems to tip. Muriel can then channel that unbound magic into granting the favor. (*See also* Muriel Taggert's Ivy Shack.)

WIZARD SLIME

Contact Agad.

An orange substance not unlike pudding, wizard slime looks unappetizing, but no other substance can equal its ability to draw out poison from infected tissue.

> Running toward danger is foolhardy. . . . But so is closing your eyes to it. Many perils become less dangerous once you understand their potential hazards.
>
> —Grandma Sorenson

WRAITH

These shadowy, spectral figures inspire great fear and leave a penetrating chill in their wake. They cannot be illuminated with a flashlight. Their whole beings seem to swallow light, leaving them indistinct and hard to see.

> Each human being has significant potential for light and darkness. Over a lifetime, we get a lot of practice leaning toward one or the other. Having made different choices, a renowned hero could have been a wretched villain.
>
> —GRANDPA SORENSON

They make great gifts. S. S.

WYVERN

Known for their speed, these dangerous beasts resemble dragons but have wolfish heads, bat-like wings, and long black claws. *They're no match for Raxtus!*
—K.S.

YOWIE

These elusive humanoids are timid but curious and sing a melancholy song. They are spotted on occasion but will quickly retreat if too much interest is shown in them. Yowies were last seen at Obsidian Waste.

I TELL MY BEST SECRETS

ONLY TO PEOPLE I KNOW

I CAN TRUST.

Otherwise the secret becomes a rumor just like that.

—Coulter

ZOMBIE

These tenacious predators can be deadly in great numbers or if you let them corner you. Fairly inept at defending themselves, zombies are actually an endangered species. These reanimated cadavers have little intelligence and are not very quick. They can be found near graveyards and have only one drive—hunger. Satisfy that drive, and they can be quite docile.

I almost had an awesome souvenir! J.S.

What lunatic decided that when people died you should hire a taxidermist to fix them up for one final look?

—KENDRA

Demons

These nefarious creatures of the darkness come in all shapes and sizes. Some walk on two legs, some on four, some on six. Others slither, jump, or roll. Some have wings, horns, or tentacles. Others have shells, scales, quills, or fur. Many wear armor and wield deadly weapons. Some have heads like dragons, others like jackals, panthers, humans, or insects. But all are to be reckoned with as powerful and dangerous beings.

In past ages, demons almost succeeded in taking over the world, which is why many were locked away in Zzyzx, the great demon prison.

BAHUMAT

One of the four most powerful demons at Fablehaven preserve, Bahumat once possessed the land where Fablehaven was founded. He stands three times as tall as a man and has the head of a dragon, crowned by three horns. He walks upright and has three arms, three legs, and three tails. Oily black scales bristling with barbed spikes cover his body. Bahumat's magic is particularly dark and frightening. His deafening roar is like a thousand cannons firing at once. He uses a wall of shadow that spreads before him like a wave of tar and engulfs any creatures in its path, leaving them blinded.

Once Muriel was free, she helped Bahumat escape by making wishes and blowing on his knots. The chapel was destroyed in the process. He was again recaptured when Kendra summoned a giant fairy army. They used golden ropes and finally buried the demon with Muriel beneath a flowering hill where the Forgotten Chapel once stood.

"Nobody is going to mess with Hostess," DOREN SAID. "Not on my watch."

For centuries, Bahumat terrorized the natives of the region until a group of Europeans offered to overthrow him in exchange for a claim to the lands he haunted. Aided by mighty allies and potent magic, the Europeans successfully subdued and imprisoned the demon. In 1826, Bahumat almost escaped when the prison that held him was damaged, but he was successfully moved to the basement of a church, now known as the Forgotten Chapel. He was there imprisoned in much the same way as Muriel was, with a web of knotted ropes.

Good riddance to both of them! — K.S.

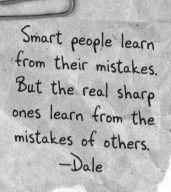

Smart people learn from their mistakes. But the real sharp ones learn from the mistakes of others.
—Dale

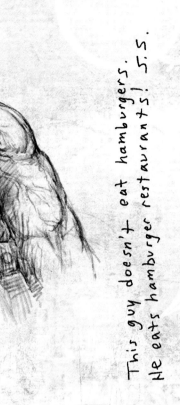

This guy doesn't eat hamburgers. He eats hamburger restaurants! S.S.

BROGO

One of the three sons of Gorgrog, king of the demons, this shirtless mountain of a man has an iron collar about his neck and a steel mask over his face. His elephantine skin and thick layers of blubber ripple as his rotund muscles gather and release. In one hand he clutches a gigantic mace, in the other a tremendous morning star.

He's been known to attack castles unaided. Unarguably the strongest demon in history, this brute has single-handedly felled forests, smashed monuments, crushed armies, and destroyed cities.

DIN BIDOR

This demon resembles an enormous wolf with crooked fangs that protrude like tusks and fur as dark as ink. Darkness and his victim's fear increase his size. He has been known to travel with Lxyria.

The best way to avoid being the slave is to be the master.
—THE SPHINX

GORGROG

King of the demons, Gorgrog is not as tall as his son Brogo but is just as formidable. His enormous humanoid figure is covered in thick fur, and his bullish head is topped with a tremendous rack of contorted antlers, encircled at the base by an iron crown. His roar is enough to completely drown out the clamor of a large battle. His weapon of choice is a huge, elaborate sword, its edges bristling with spikes and serrations. He drags his victim's corpses on the ground behind him, affixed to his wide belt by black chains.

The bigger they are . . . —K.S.

GRAULAS

This aged demon was once one of the most feared and respected demons in the world. He is demonic royalty, and long ago he served as left hand to Gorgrog, the demon king. As exuding terror is part of his nature, his presence inspires a paralyzing horror in humans. Once extremely powerful, over time he has deteriorated into a decrepit echo of his former grandeur.

You got what you deserved! —Seth

what a loser, you slimy, shadowy lump of mush! -Seth

KURISOCK

More shadow than substance, Kurisock must bind himself to a host in order to interact with the mortal world. In return for a borrowed physical form, he imbues his host with power. Depending on the host, the results can be terrifying. This demon is bound by oath not to pass beyond the borders of Fablehaven, but he can partner with entities outside the domain. Kurisock has never been seen but is known to live in the tar pit.

LENA IS THE BRAVEST, MOST SELFLESS, MOST BEAUTIFUL PERSON IN THE WORLD. I WILL MISS HER—UNTIL WE MEET AGAIN.
—PATTON

LXYRIA

This muscular woman with four arms and the body of a serpent is a greater demon and a mentor to witches and hags.

LYCERNA

This female reptilian demon has overthrown all order at the Rio Branco preserve in Brazil.

To fall from greatness, from the dizziest heights to the deepest depths, knowing one might have prevented it, certain one will never reclaim what one has lost, cripples the will. Life holds no more meaning than one chooses to impose, and I quit pretending long ago.
—Graulas

NAGI LUNA

Arguably the most feared demon outside of Zzyzx, Nagi Luna can see things beyond her ordinary field of vision and can control the bodies of those who are too weak to resist her. She also has the power to turn the dust of the earth into enchanted items, such as fatally poisonous needles.

Though at first glance she appears to be a frail, old woman with a woolen shawl draped over her hunched form, a more attentive observer will note that her yellow eyes are a strangely slanted shape, her thin earlobes sag almost to her shoulders, and her demented grin reveals ragged, inflamed gums. Her blotchy skin is purple and maroon, and she has gray claws at the end of her gnarled hands.

Or you can call her Dog Breath! - Seth

Under no circumstances should you let her into your mind.

OLLOCH THE GLUTTON

This froglike demon has been transformed by a spell into a polished, green-speckled-jade toad figurine. He stands upright instead of on all fours, his short arms folded across his chest. He remains in a petrified state, inert, until somebody feeds him. Once he bites the hand that feeds him he begins to gradually awaken, driven by an insatiable appetite. The more he eats, the more he grows. As his size increases, so does his power, and he does not stop eating until he consumes the person who initially awakened him.

Olloch uses his myriad tongues to snatch his victims—like a frog catching a fly—pulling them into his mouth to devour them.

Do NOT FEED HIM!!! You'll regret it if you do! —Seth

Olloch nearly destroyed Fablehaven! His statue lies dormant on the preserve. Remarkably, Seth survived after being consumed, but he doesn't want anyone to know how he did it. He says he needs to have some secrets if he's going to become the world's next great adventurer just like Patton Burgess. He's totally going to end up in a body cast! —Kendra

> **EVIL** likes darkness . . .
> *because* **EVIL** likes to hide.
>
> —Grandma Sorenson

OROGORO

The eldest son of Gorgrog, this hulking, shaggy demon has antlers like his father and inspires similar terror as he wields his enormous battle-axe. One may distinguish him by his missing foot, lost to the longsword blade of astrid captain Gilgarol.

ZORAT THE PLAGUEMAN

Considerably taller than a regular person, this demon's pale skin is pocked with sores. His long, spindly arms and legs give him spidery proportions. Saliva drips from his slack mouth, and yellowy pus clots his red eyes.

> # I MADE TWO SIMPLE RULES,
> ## YOU UNDERSTOOD THEM,
> # AND YOU BROKE THEM.
>
> Just because I chose not to share all my reasons for making the rules, you think you should escape punishment?
>
> —Grandpa Sorenson

DRAGONWATCH

Dear Kendra and Seth,

It is with a heavy heart that I write these words, almost against my will. The wizard Agad recently informed me of unrest at Wyrmroost. Not long ago, Celebrant gained control of the sanctuary in return for his aid against the demons, and already Wyrmroost is in danger of falling. Agad needs me to go to Wyrmroost temporarily to function as a joint-caretaker with Celebrant, and I will require your unique talents in order to succeed. I would not let you be drawn into these matters if they were not of critical importance.

In ancient times, dragons became the ultimate threat to the mythical world. At the height of the Age of Dragons, it appeared that dragons might not only gain dominion over all magical races, but could potentially overrun the nonmagical world as well.

Dragonwatch was a group of wizards, enchantresses, dragon slayers, and others who banded together to stand against the dragons and, together, they eventually confined the majority of them to dragon sanctuaries. That effort began the practice of establishing preserves for magical creatures.

Though mostly inactive for centuries, some of the key remaining members of Dragonwatch have recently been contacted by Agad. Though I don't know all the details yet, the latest subversive activities by the dragons goes beyond the situation at Wyrmroost. At this time, the full scale of the threat has yet to be determined, but our current orders are clear—to keep Wyrmroost from falling.

I will make no efforts to compel you to join me. The danger will be extreme, and so your involvement in this crisis can only be voluntary.

Reluctantly,
Stan Sorenson

THE SOMBER KNIGHT

The Somber Knight has not emerged from his subterranean keep for centuries, and nobody has sought him out. Once considered the last line of defense against a dragon uprising at Wyrmroost, some question whether he remains alive.

DROMADUS

Unlike most dragon kings, Dromadus lost his station without losing his life. After Ranjimar the Terrible defeated him during the Age of Dragons, Dromadus yielded and went into exile. None know his present location, but rumor has it that he lives in isolation, hibernating most of the time.

ISADORE

Once a dragon, Isadore surrendered her powers to become a powerful enchantress. A mysterious figure who seems drawn to disaster, she has a close relationship with a shadowy black dragon named Basirus.

Dragons

Dragons are quite possibly the most powerful race of magical creatures. Much like humans, they have a wide array of personalities. Some believe in justice. Others are wicked. Few have much regard for human life. Highly intelligent, dragons have their own unique language but often speak hundreds of additional tongues. No two dragons are identical. They have diverse appearances, various breath weapons, and distinct spell-casting abilities.

These supernatural predators are protected by scales harder than stone and bones as strong as adamant. Each dragon has a unique arsenal of powers at its disposal, beyond its teeth, tail, and claws. Some can spin webs, and others can live underwater where they use dense clouds of ink to confuse their prey. And of course their spectacular breath weapons like breathing fire, lightning, or acid are famous for good reason.

The oldest dragons are among the most ancient creatures on the planet. Dragons live for thousands of years, can grow to the size of hills, have frighteningly keen intellects, and benefit from deep magic woven into every fiber of their bodies. The remains of a dragon are sacred. Their bones are lighter and stronger than almost any substance and can neither be destroyed by time nor the elements. Only other dragons can properly dispose of them.

Almost all mortals who try to converse with a dragon will find themselves instantly transfixed and rendered powerless. A dragon tamer can avoid this effect and may actually hold a conversation, but nobody really tames a dragon. They are so accustomed to overpowering all other beings that when dragons find a human they cannot break they are intriged. Such humans are referred to as a dragon brother.

Much like becoming fairykind—though even more rare—a dragon brother is essentially adopted by the dragons and seen as one of their own. A dragon brother can speak their language and becomes stronger and faster than normal.

It's a dangerous game for humans, but sometimes dragons will grant favors to such individuals, including allowing them to live. Dragons see ordinary humans as mice—not a real threat, but a potential annoyance. If they find humans underfoot, they will most likely kill them just to keep the area tidy.

Dragons are magical from the tips of their fangs to the ends of their tails, but their tears are an especially potent ingredient for magical potions. (*See* Dragon Tears.) In addition, there is a rare weed called daughter-of-despair from which a toxin known as dragonsbane can be derived, the only venom capable of poisoning a dragon, but it is extremely hard to come by and to formulate. Although dragons have a highly developed sense of smell, they cannot detect dragonsbane.

Many mature dragons can assume human form. Most are content to transform back and forth on occasion, but in exchange for greater magic, some have transformed permanently, becoming true wizards. Such wizards were instrumental in confining dragons to the sanctuaries where most now dwell. Dragons have little fondness for those of their kind who embrace permanent humanity. A dragon prefers being a dragon and can only tolerate being human while clothed in human form. Changing back and forth can be disorienting because the form they assume affects their minds.

ARCHADIUS

Long ago, this wise dragon discovered that by permanently assuming human form, he significantly increased his magical abilities. Some other dragons followed suit. It is unknown whether he is still alive.

CAMARAT

Longer than two school busses set end-to-end, this Oriental dragon is brother to Agad and has a head like a giant lion with red-gold fur, a crimson mane, and a gold-and-red serpentine body. Eight sets of legs support his scaly body—his large feet each a hybrid of dragon claw and lion paw—and two sets of golden feathers fan out from his sides. Camarat's roar is like that of a thousand lions, and he exhales blue-white flames that can force a person to speak the truth. Camarat guards the entrance to Wyrmroost.

Cool hair.
S.S.

You're too trusting.
Too independent.
Too good of a friend,
even to one who is by
nature your enemy.
These attributes were
used against you.
—Graulas to Seth

CELEBRANT

King of the dragons, Celebrant is enormous, agile, and powerful. He resides at Wyrmroost. His impenetrable scales gleam like platinum, and all dragons consider him an unequaled physical specimen. He has five breath weapons and an arsenal of offensive spells. This dignified, majestic dragon has a mind as keen as a razor. His preferred attack is a blinding burst of white energy.

No wonder Raxtus feels like he lives in his dad's shadow.
—K.S.

CHALIZE

This young female dragon has gleaming copper scales that encase her elephant-sized body in metallic armor. A tall fin runs from the top of her fierce head to the base of her neck, a pair of shiny wings grace her sides, and her long tail extends like a whip. Offspring of the dragon Nafia, Chalize was stolen from her nest and brought to Lost Mesa.

GLOMMUS

This blind old dragon is renowned for his unique breath weapon. With this thick mist, he can put anyone and anything to sleep—even other dragons. After a slight intake of breath, his victims are instantly unconscious. Glommus has a huge gray head and a slow, deep voice. He is one of the protectors of the dragon temple at Wyrmroost.

IF DRAGONS WEREN'T
FREAKY,
THEY'D BE . . .
disappointing.
—SETH

NAFIA

Nafia is the size of a whale, her body covered with scales of shining blue and violet.

Elaborate spines and ridges project from a head larger than a car. Her eyes are like jewels lit by a radiant inner fire, enhancing her mesmerizing gaze. This dragon typically ate her offspring, but one of them, Chalize, was rescued from this fate when, as an egg, she was stolen and taken to Lost Mesa.

Nafia's human avatar, Nyssa, is a tall, beautiful woman with aristocratic features—chiseled cheekbones, flawless skin, imperious eyes, and a lithe frame. Her most striking feature is her lustrous, silvery-blue hair. Though much older in reality, she appears somewhere in her midtwenties and carries herself with a casual confidence.

NAVAROG

Navarog is widely acknowledged as one of the most corrupt and dangerous of all dragons. Recognized as a prince among demons, he sold his honor long ago in exchange for power. An armor of dark, oily scales covers his sides and back, and his belly appears encrusted with black jewels. Cruel spikes protrude from his massive tail and along his spine, his claws curve like huge scythes, and his eyes burn like magma.

RANTICUS

One of the dragons who never sought refuge in a sanctuary, Ranticus, rotten to the core, is numbered among the twenty lost dragons and is rumored to dwell in the vast networks of caverns below Lost Mesa. A band of goblins worships Ranticus, bringing him tributes of food and treasure.

 # RAXTUS

I ♡ Raxtus! BFF! —Kendra

As an egg, Raxtus was rescued from a cockatrice and raised by fairies. He is reportedly the only dragon in the world who, because of his relationship with the Fairy Queen, can approach her shrines. One of his magical powers is his ability to become invisible. Though he was sired by Celebrant, the dragon king, Raxtus has a reputation as a weakling. Unlike his father and half brothers, he is shy and introverted.

Much smaller than most dragons his age, Raxtus has gleaming armor of silvery-white scales and a head as bright as polished chrome. His voice sounds somewhat like a confident teenager's but is surprisingly rich and full. His lean, sleek build is designed for speed. His magical breath enables things to grow. Raxtus's avatar is a twelve-inch scrawny fairy with elaborate metallic butterfly wings and shaggy silver hair.

> Good choices are not always safe choices. Many worthy choices involve risk. Some require courage.
> —PATTON

SILETTA

Lacking visible scales, Siletta looks like a giant salamander with translucent skin. Networks of dark blue veins tangle with her purple and green organs, all of which are visible beneath her semitransparent hide. Large enough to swallow a car, her wide mouth contains multiple rows of slim, pale teeth that are sharp and slightly curved. This unique dragon was thought to be either legend or long dead. Siletta is a living fountainhead of the most potent venoms ever known. Her breath, her flesh, her blood, her tears, her excretions—every part of her contains a deadly poison. Siletta spits an acidic tarlike substance. One of the only known protections against her many poisons is a unicorn's horn.

I thought we were goners. —K.S.

CAN YOU SEE

THE POWER EMOTION HAS
TO DISTORT OUR OUTLOOK?

MAKES YOU WONDER,

---

did you HAVE a bad day, or
did you MAKE IT a bad day?

—TANU

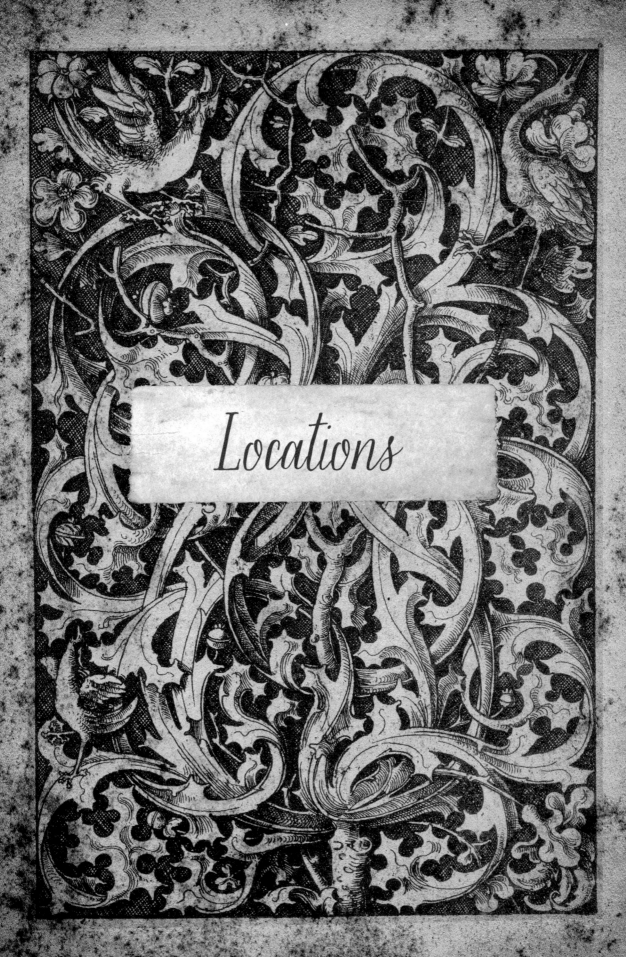

Locations

BROWNIE HOLE

The brownies at Fablehaven use underground tunnels to reach their secret dwellings far beneath the earth. The entrances are covered with soft, loose dirt, and roots poke through the first several yards of the tunnel's walls but gradually give way to smooth walls and a level floor. The comparatively crude tunnels eventually lead to the tidy doors of the brownie homes. (*See also* Brownie.)

DRAGON SANCTUARIES

The seven dragon sanctuaries were the first preserves created for magical creatures and are unlike other preserves where visitors are protected by caretakers. Entering a dragon sanctuary is like entering the wild, as these sanctuaries were founded as homes for creatures too large and powerful to cohabitate with the beings at the more traditional preserves.

Few people know about these sanctuaries, and almost nobody knows the locations of all seven.

It is rumored that four of the seven dragon sanctuaries welcome human visitors once they secure permission from the sanctuaries' caretakers. The other three sanctuaries are considerably less hospitable.

Frosted Peaks = the Himalayas?

DRAGON TEMPLES

The three dragon temples are hidden inside the three forbidden dragon sanctuaries. Each temple houses the preeminent valuables of all treasure hoards—the most precious and powerful items amassed by the dragons of the world. And each temple contains a certain talisman the dragons wish to keep out of mortal hands. It was partly in exchange for these three talismans that dragons agreed to come to the sanctuaries in the first place. (*See also* Sage's Gauntlets.)

WYRMROOST

One of the dragon sanctuaries, Wyrmroost is located just north of Montana and is protected by a magical barrier that extends a mile into the sky. It is inaccessible without a key—the first horn of a unicorn—that unlocks the main gate. Though this stronghold is timeworn and dreary, it is protected by one of the most powerful distracter spells in the world.

Appearing to be an abandoned castle, Wyrmroost has a gray stone wall with round towers at the corners and a raised drawbridge in the center, its dark timbers studded with iron. The broad, crenellated wall reaches approximately twenty feet high, the corner towers an extra ten feet taller. None of the buildings beyond the wall are much higher. No visible guards or sentries man its battlements, but the dragon Camarat is always watching, ready to intercept any intruders.

Agad, the wizard, is the last known caretaker.

This place holds bad memories.
— K.S.
☹

THE FORGOTTEN CHAPEL

This dilapidated house of worship was destroyed when the demon Bahumat attempted to escape from his imprisonment in the basement. The old church house was leveled and buried when the fairy army defeated Bahumat.

THE GREAT MARSH OF FABLEHAVEN

This mysterious, large expanse of soupy terrain is one of the most perilous, least explored areas of the Fablehaven preserve. An abundance of moss and vines burden the trees, and shreds of mist swirl near the ground. The warm air reeks of decay. Fuzzy mushrooms and slimy rocks decorate half-drowned islands. Various paths run through the marsh, some real, some counterfeit. Explorers must beware of the swamp hag, who uses false trails to lure travelers to their demise.

SAFE HUT

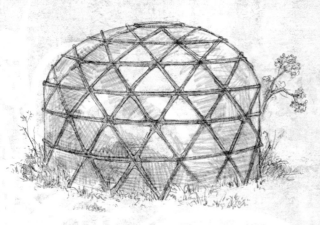

A safe hut is a geodesic dome comprised of a triangular grid of glass and steel, similar to the interlocking metal bars on a playground, and is placed in some of the more threatening areas of the preserve to provide refuge for travelers. The only opening to the structure is through a small hatch on the side. No creature can enter the hut uninvited. One safe hut is located in the Great Marsh.

GRUNHOLD

Located on the far side of Fablehaven's marshlands, this home of the centaurs is surrounded by a protective ring of stone. The centaurs live in a proud, private society and will slay any who venture onto their lands. Manicured paths wind through the vineyards and orchards, around hedges and earthworks, beneath arched trellises, up ramps, and over small, decorative bridges. Off to the side of the city, shadowy tunnels extend into the hillside. The Soul of Grunhold keeps this thriving community alive as a haven for these creatures of light during times of darkness.

Or a banana? Still so funny. —Seth

HALL OF DREAD

The darkness of this eerily cold corridor is almost palpable. Eight doors, four on each side, bar the escape of imprisoned wraiths and other sinister beings. Each of these equally spaced doors is crafted from solid iron and embossed with archaic symbols and pictograms. Each has a keyhole and a closed peephole. Nobody visits the Hall of Dread for fun.

Except maybe me! - Seth

I BUILT A SHORT PIER FROM ONE OF THE PAVILIONS
THAT LEADS TO THE BOAT HOUSE. THERE ARE 3 BOATS
INSIDE: 2 LARGE ROWBOATS, ONE SLIGHTLY BROADER
THAN THE OTHER, AND A SMALLER PADDLEBOAT.
SEVERAL OARS HANG ON THE WALL. TO OPEN THE
BOAT HOUSE DOOR SIMPLY USE THE CRANK.

THE HIDDEN POND

Less than a mile from the main house at Fablehaven lies a large pond surrounded by a wooden boardwalk with twelve white pavilions. The sacred island at the center of the pond is prohibited to mortals because it contains a shrine dedicated to the Fairy Queen. To set foot on the island means certain death. However, the pavilions and the lawns around the pond provide a welcome haven for creatures of light, including humans.

Without drinking the milk, mortal visitors will see butterflies, hummingbirds, parrots, monkeys, goats, and peacocks wandering the grounds of this enchanting abode. After drinking the milk, the true identities of these creatures come into view.

WARNING: IF YOU CHOOSE TO TAKE A BOAT ONTO THE POND BEWARE OF THE TAUNTING NAIADS. THEY WILL TRY TO TIP YOUR BOAT AND PURPOSEFULLY DROWN YOU! AT THIS POINT YOU ARE PROBABLY WONDERING WHAT KIND OF PERSON WOULD CHOOSE TO WILLINGLY ROW ONTO THE POND KNOWING THAT GRAVE DANGER AWAITS. MY ANSWER IS SIMPLE. LOVE CAN BE A POWERFUL AND SOMETIMES UNREASONABLE MOTIVATOR. — PATTON BURGESS

THE INVERTED TOWER

This structure serves as a vault for the hidden artifact at Fablehaven.

Located in the Revenant's grove, the entrance to the tower lies in the middle of a clearing where stands a sizable, raised platform of reddish stone flecked with black and gold. At the center of this spacious platform is a round socket surrounded by multiple circular grooves that radiate out like the rings around a bull's-eye. To gain access, a key must be inserted into the socket. Once the key is in place, the outer rings drop away one at a time, until a conical staircase is formed, which leads down to a chamber.

This first chamber of three is not much larger than the widest ring of stone, its floor a single slab of bedrock. There is nothing in the chamber except a pair of doors at opposite ends. One section of the chamber's wall is covered in writings in various languages, including a few repeated messages in English and fairy languages. Behind both doors are false staircases. Along the wall is an invisible entrance with a genuine set of stairs leading to the next chamber.

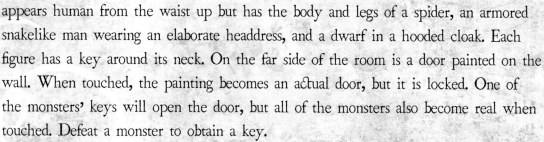

The second chamber is large and circular. White stones set in the domed ceiling provide illumination. Deep, golden sand—some of which is quicksand—covers the floor. Monsters are depicted on the walls of this chamber—a blue woman with six arms and the body of a serpent, a minotaur, a huge cyclops, a dark man who appears human from the waist up but has the body and legs of a spider, an armored snakelike man wearing an elaborate headdress, and a dwarf in a hooded cloak. Each figure has a key around its neck. On the far side of the room is a door painted on the wall. When touched, the painting becomes an actual door, but it is locked. One of the monsters' keys will open the door, but all of the monsters also become real when touched. Defeat a monster to obtain a key.

Once the correct key is used, the door will open to reveal another stairway that descends to the third chamber. On the floor is a complex mosaic depicting primates engaged in an enormous battle in tall trees. The mosaic's perspective is from the ground looking up and creates a disorienting effect. The instant the chamber is entered, the primates come to life, frenzied beasts intent on killing.

Once the apes are defeated, however, a passageway on the opposite side of the room opens to yet another stairway, which in turn opens to the fourth and final room, where a glass, black cat guardian sits atop a pedestal, a key hanging around the feline's neck. Once this guardian is defeated, the hidden artifact will be revealed.

Black Cat Guardian

In order to pass by this guardian, we had to take each of its nine lives. With each death, the cat was reincarnated and became something more fearsome and vicious. When one incarnation was slain, its carcass melted or boiled or bulged with new life. The cat was activated by touch, and when the key was removed from its neck, it became frighteningly possessive.

- The first incarnation: a life-sized, glass black cat.
- The second incarnation: a super-sized, menacing feline.
- The third incarnation: a lynx with long sharp claws, tufted ears, and intimidating teeth.
- The fourth incarnation: a larger and more aggressive version of the lynx.
- The fifth incarnation: a panther.
- The sixth incarnation: a larger and more ferocious panther.
- The seventh incarnation: an even larger panther, as tall as a horse, with dagger-like claws and saber-toothed fangs. Four writhing venomous black serpents also sprouted from the panther's shoulders.
- The eighth incarnation: no serpents, but another head formed, and both heads spat black sludge that burned like acid.
- The ninth and final incarnation: a terrifying, gargantuan cat with twelve serpents along its back. It had three heads, three heavy tails, wings, and also spat acid. It took everything we had to slay this final version. --Kendra

This would make an awesome video game! - Seth

MAGICAL PRESERVES

Magical preserves are the final refuges for many of the world's ancient and wonderful mythical species and were created to prevent these amazing beings from passing out of existence. Of the thirty-seven preserves, several are known to man. Magical preserves can be found in various climates, from Antarctica to Indonesia, including the Arizona desert and the rain forests of Brazil. All are homes to different mythical creatures. A giant walrus presides over the preserve in Greenland.

Among the thirty-seven active preserves in the world, five are unmarked because they are the repositories of perilous magical artifacts. Few know about these unmarked preserves thanks to a worldwide network of dedicated souls who have kept them secret for thousands of years. These guardians are backed by ancient fortunes held in trust. These five preserves are listed here:

FABLEHAVEN

Located in Connecticut, Fablehaven was founded in 1711 and is one of the newest of the secret preserves. Long ago, the land where Fablehaven now stands was possessed by the powerful demon Bahumat. For centuries, he terrorized the natives. They learned to avoid certain areas, yet even with these precautions, the vicinity was never truly safe. The natives made whatever offerings the demon required but they continually lived in fear.

When a group of Europeans offered to overthrow the demon in exchange for a claim to the lands, the local leaders consented. Aided by mighty allies and potent magic, the Europeans successfully subdued and imprisoned the demon. Some years later, they founded Fablehaven.

In the early 1800s, a community composed chiefly of extended family populated this preserve. They built a number of dwellings around a large, sturdy mansion, which stands to this day. The current caretakers for this preserve are the Sorensons.

Apprentice Caretaker: Seth Sorenson

And Kendra!

Midsummer's Eve.

Four nights per year, the boundaries on the preserves that define where different entities can venture dissolve, and all the creatures run wild. One such night, Midsummer's Eve, is the summer solstice and signals the longest day of the year. This is a holiday of riotous abandon for the whimsical creatures of Fablehaven.

The winter solstice and the two equinoxes are the other three times of the year for such revelry, but Midsummer's Eve tends to be the rowdiest of them all. One may gain protection from the riotous creatures with magical salts, herbs, fairy milk, and most of all, jack-o'-lanterns (fairy lanterns), which have long been among the surest protections from mythical creatures with dubious intentions.

The Register

The register is a book that controls access to Fablehaven. When a visitor's name is written in the register, the spells protecting Fablehaven from intruders will no longer bother the person. Without recording a name in the register, access to Fablehaven becomes nearly impossible.

It's fun to read through the old guests.

K.S.

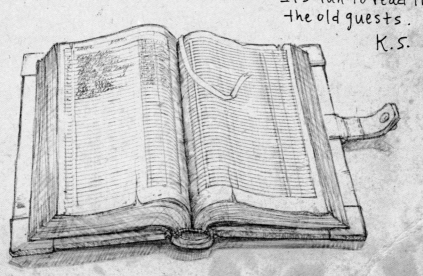

LIVING MIRAGE

Located in eastern Turkey, this preserve houses the Font of Immortality and is overseen by the Sphinx. It is the most successfully hidden preserve of all five. There are pyramids on this preserve, the main structure housing both living space for the preserve's caretaker and an underground dungeon that holds the infamous demon Nagi Luna.

Chimeras, dwarves, steppe giants, karkadanns, manticores, and harpies are some of Living Mirage's residents.

Not a fun place—but I did meet Bracken there. K. S.

LOST MESA

Located in the desert of Arizona, this preserve's landscape consists of sunbaked dirt and turquoise sagebrush, with saguaros scattered here and there. Within this preserve is the Painted Mesa, an enormous plateau with striking bands of white, yellow, orange, and red coloring its steep sides, where many of the mesa's magical creatures reside.

Lost Mesa is different from many other preserves in that it has always been managed by a female caretaker—Rosa comes from the Pueblo culture, in which women inherit the property. The artifact hidden on this preserve is (unknown.)

Some of the magical creatures found on Lost Mesa are jackalopes, zombies, fairies, kachinas, and even a dragon.

It was unknown! Patton got to it first, but I got to it second!! :)

OBSIDIAN WASTE

The Obsidian Waste is located in Australia. Some of the occupants of the Obsidian Waste are yowies, thylacines, fairies, and zombies.

Part of the Obsidian Waste preserve, the Dreamstone is a large obsidian rock formation laced with potent magic designed to trap anyone who enters. It is a geological marvel that from the outside looks like a black mountain that was somehow sculpted into a glossy brick. Its black surface reflects light, producing a rainbow.

A secret artifact is hidden inside the Dreamstone, though relic hunters must overcome a series of formidable challenges in order to obtain it, including crossing a boiling body of water, solving a baffling maze, and obtaining a key from the neck of a mechanical lion.

RIO BRANCO

This secret preserve is located in Brazil. The caretakers of Rio Branco have a key to a vault where a secret artifact is kept. This vault is located near a point called Tres Cabecas, where three huge boulders overlook the main river. Umite sprites, known for their magical wax, inhabit this preserve.

GREENLAND
PRESERVE

•DRAGON SANCTUARY
Wymroost
North America
•Fablehaven

•Lost Mesa

Af

South
America
•
Rio Branco

N

nw   ne

W   E

sw   se

S

•ANTARCTICA PRESERVE #2

Antar

Asia

Europe

Living Mirage

Himalayan
Preserve

South Asian
Preserve

Tibetan Sanctuary

Indonesia Preserve

Timor Preserve

Australia
Obsidian Waste

Antarctica Preserve #1

MURIEL TAGGERT'S IVY SHACK

This dilapidated structure, overgrown by thick ivy and constructed around a large tree stump, functions as Muriel Taggert's prison at Fablehaven. Muriel sits inside, gnawing at the magical, knotted rope that binds her for her crimes. (*See also* Witch.)

She never lured me in there. Probably a good thing. S.S.

The curse of mortality. You spend the first portion of your life learning, growing stronger, more capable. And then, through no fault of your own, your body begins to fail. You regress. Strong limbs become feeble, keen senses grow dull, hardy constitutions deteriorate. Beauty withers. Organs quit. You remember yourself in your prime, and wonder where that person went. As your wisdom and experience are peaking, your traitorous body becomes a prison.

—Lena

OLD MANOR

Once the main house and center of the Fablehaven community, this impressive manor, surprisingly intact compared to the road and the other dwellings that surround it, is three stories tall, with four large pillars in the front and a circular driveway. Flowering vines twist around the pillars and climb the gray walls. Weeds and young trees grow up from the flagstone road leading to the manor. Off to the side of this path are the decaying remnants of a humble cabin and a few smaller shelters.

SEVEN KINGDOMS OF THE NIPSIES

Radiating out from a central pond, an elaborate irrigation system composed of canals, aqueducts, pools, and dams connects seven sprawling communities of dense habitations bristling with tiny castles, mansions, factories, warehouses, shops, mills, theaters, arenas, and bridges. The architecture of the miniature kingdoms is complex and varied, and incorporates soaring spires, swooping rooftops, spiraling towers, fragile arches, cartoonish chimneys, colorful canopies, columned walkways, multitiered gardens, and glistening domes. The smallest of the fairy folk built their empires using the finest wood and stone. Precious metals and gemstones add a gleam to many of their fanciful structures. (*See also* Nipsy.)

SHRINE TO THE FAIRY QUEEN

Protected by naiads, the shrine to the Fairy Queen at Fablehaven sits on a small island, not seventy paces in circumference, at the center of a sizeable pond. Although the island lacks trees, it has many shrubs and a curious, small spring that burbles from the ground near the center of the island. At the head of this stream sits a finely carved fairy statue, no taller than two inches, which rests on a white pedestal. A small silver bowl sits in front of it. No mortal is permitted on this hallowed ground.

CREATURES OF WHIMSY ARE NOT SOLELY CONFINED TO THE PRESERVES. THE BLINDNESS OF MORTALS CAN BE A BLESSING. TAKE CARE WHERE YOU LOOK.
—GRANDPA SORENSON

TAURAN MAZE

The Soul of Grunhold lies at the heart of the Tauran Maze, deep inside a hill topped by warding stones. The Tauran Maze's protective, invisible walls are laced with fatal spells. Any intruder who touches them will be instantly struck down. Such contact also raises an alarm. At the heart of the unsolvable maze awaits Udnar the mountain troll as a final obstacle.

The entrance to the maze lies beneath the southernmost warding stone, which is too large to move and is bound in place by a spell. However, each night, two hours before dawn, the warding stones march for an hour, trading places. For that hour of the night, while the stones are marching, the entrance to the maze lies uncovered.

THE VALLEY OF THE FOUR HILLS

This large, open valley has a rounded hill at each corner. Tall brush covers the ground, mingling with prickly weeds. A dark stand of trees looms at the far end of the valley between the two largest hills. There is almost no undergrowth in the grove, just rank upon rank of gray pillars supporting its leafy canopy. Many areas of Fablehaven carry terrible curses and are protected by ghastly fiends. The grove in the valley of the four hills is one of the most dreaded.

ZZYZX

Located in the Atlantic on the Shoreless Isle, somewhere southwest of Bermuda, Zzyzx is the great prison where literally thousands of the most powerful demons from every age of this world are incarcerated. Zzyzx lies inside the central mountain—a huge dome of rock—and is nearly impossible to find and less possible to access. Along with other defenses, massive distracter spells drive away attention. Ships have a history of vanishing in this vicinity, which is also known as the Bermuda Triangle. The only way to access the prison is to bring the five ancient artifacts together and kill the Eternals. Were this ever to happen, the result would be catastrophic.

The wizards who built this prison were aware of the principle that everything with a beginning must have an end. This also includes magic, which, like everything

Real end-of-the-world stuff... —Seth

else, eventually becomes unstable and unravels. These wizards knew that constructing an impenetrable prison was doomed to failure, and so they focused on making it extraordinarily complicated to open. Their goal was to make Zzyzx *nearly* impenetrable, as close to perfect as possible without crossing the line.

Because there *is* a way to open Zzyzx, the magic that binds the demons there is more potent.

Not your typical island resort.

K.S.

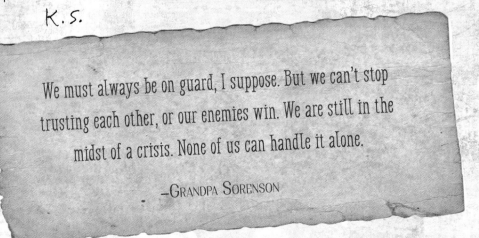

We must always be on guard, I suppose. But we can't stop trusting each other, or our enemies win. We are still in the midst of a crisis. None of us can handle it alone.

—Grandpa Sorenson

MAKING MISTAKES IS PART OF LEARNING TO CHOOSE WELL.

No way around it.

CHOICES ARE THRUST UPON US,
AND WE DON'T ALWAYS GET THINGS RIGHT.

Even postponing or avoiding a decision can become
a choice that carries heavy consequences.

Mistakes can be painful—sometimes they cause
irrevocable harm—but welcome to Earth.

POOR CHOICES ARE PART OF GROWING UP, AND PART OF LIFE.

YOU WILL MAKE BAD CHOICES, AND YOU WILL BE
AFFECTED BY THE POOR CHOICES OF OTHERS.

We must rise above such things.

–PATTON

Wizards

Though few known wizards now survive, all true wizards were once dragons. Long ago, a wise dragon named Archadius discovered that by permanently assuming human form, he significantly increased his magical abilities. Those dragons most interested in magic followed suit.

Dragons have little fondness for those dragon-turned-wizards who embraced permanent humanity. To some extent they view wizards as weak, to some extent they are jealous, and to some extent they blame wizards for the general decline of dragons, because wizards were among the greatest dragon slayers and played an instrumental role in confining the dragons to sanctuaries.

I'm dumb, but I'm not stupid.
—SETH

AGAD

This plump, elderly man with a flowing gray beard, black cloak, and jeweled rings on his fingers is custodian of Wyrmroost and one of the five wizards who created Zzyzx.

MIRAV

This old wizard from India has a melodic voice and wears a cape and a turban. He has golden skin and his braided beard is decorated with beads, bones, and bits of twine. With every step, he leaves behind a flaming blue-and-green footprint. An evil wizard, Mirav is a leader among the Society of the Evening Star. He can only come out at night because direct sunlight will kill him.

THE SOCIETY OF THE EVENING STAR

Once thought to be extinct, the Society of the Evening Star has recently been on the rise. Members of this organization consort with demons and practitioners of the black arts and are intent on destroying all of the preserves in order to acquire the five artifacts and open Zzyzx.

The Society chose its name because "The evening star ushers in the night." Members of the Society mask their true intentions with rhetoric, alleging that the various creatures of darkness are wrongfully imprisoned. They also argue that the covenants of the preserves create artificial rules that upset the natural order of things, trapping mythical creatures in artificial settings.

The Society considers the majority of humanity expendable and believes chaos and bloodshed are preferable to just regulations. If the Society ever succeeds in its goal of opening Zzyzx, the results could be apocalyptic.

MORISANT

Morisant was the eldest of the wizards at Zzyzx and owner of the sword Vasilis. Once the chief architect of Zzyzx, this wizard turned himself into one of the undead in order to prolong his life. Now a zombie with a decaying, corroded body, this once-powerful wizard admits that his pitiful state is a result of hubris.

Morisant believed he was above the rules that applied to others. As his quest for power spun out of control, he became a threat to the safety of the world, and his most trusted colleagues were forced to put him in prison. Though he has now recognized his mistakes and mastered his inability to slake his appetites, his nature is fundamentally corrupted. He wishes to undo the perversions he has wrought before it is too late.

I'm not going to lie. This dude had an army of the undead that freaked me out!! — Seth

INDEX

A

Adamant Breastplate · 2
Agad · 110
Alcetaur · 20
Anti-Eavesdropping Candle · 3
Apparition · 20
Archadius · 79
Astrid · 20

B

Bahumat · 66–67
Basilisk · 21
Becoming Fairykind · 27
Black Cat Guardian · 95
Blix · 21
Bottled Messages · 3
Brogo · 68
Brownie · 22
Brownie Hole · 88
Bubda (hermit troll) · 57

C

Camarat · 79
Celebrant · 80
Centaur · 23
Chalize · 80
Chimera · 23
Chokepod · 42
Chronometer · 6

Cliff Troll · 56
Cormac (leprechaun) · 40
Courage potion · 10
Cyclops · 23

D

Demons · 65
Din Bidor · 68
Distracter Spell · 4
Doren (satyr) · 52
Dragons · 77–78
Dragon Sanctuaries · 88
Dragon Tears · 4
Dragon Temples · 89
Drumant · 24
Dryad · 46
Dullion (golem) · 32
Dwarf · 24

E

Enlarger potion · 10
Eternals, the · 24
Eye Drops · 4

F

Fablehaven · 96
Fairy · 25–26
Fairy Queen · 27

Firedrake ❧ 29
Fire-Resistant potion (Dragon Insurance) ❧ 11
Flash Powder ❧ 4
Fog Giant ❧ 31
Font of Immortality ❧ 6
Forgotten Chapel, the ❧ 90

❧ G ❧

Gargoyle ❧ 29
Gaseous-State Potion ❧ 11
Giant ❧ 30
Giant Walrus ❧ 31
Glommus ❧ 81
Goblin ❧ 32
Golem ❧ 32
Gorgrog ❧ 69
Graulas ❧ 69
Great Marsh of Fablehaven, the ❧ 90
Griffin ❧ 34–35
Grunhold ❧ 91

❧ H ❧

Hall of Dread ❧ 92
Hamadryad ❧ 46
Harpy ❧ 36
Hawkbear ❧ 36
Hermit Troll ❧ 57
Hidden Pond, the ❧ 93
Holly Wand ❧ 5
Hugo (golem) ❧ 33
Hydra ❧ 36

❧ I ❧

Imp ❧ 37
Inverted Tower, the ❧ 94

❧ J ❧

Jackalope ❧ 37
Jinn ❧ 38
Jinn Harp Fairy ❧ 28

❧ K ❧

Kachina ❧ 39
Karkadann ❧ 39
Key to the Inverted Tower ❧ 5
Keys to Zzyzx ❧ 5
Knapsack ❧ 8
Kobold ❧ 39
Kurisock ❧ 70

❧ L ❧

Lady Luck ❧ 8
Lammasu ❧ 40
Leprechaun ❧ 40
Lich ❧ 41
Limberjack ❧ 41
Living Mirage ❧ 98
Lost Mesa ❧ 98
Lotus Blossom ❧ 42
Lxyria ❧ 70
Lycanthrope ❧ 41
Lycerna ❧ 70

❧ M ❧

Magic Glove ❧ 8
Magic Salt ❧ 9
Magical Plants ❧ 42
Magical Preserves ❧ 96
Manticore ❧ 44
Mental-Pain potion ❧ 11
Mesopotamian Triclops ❧ 23
Midsummer's Eve ❧ 97

Milch Cow   44
Minotaur   45
Mirav   110
Morisant   111
Mountain Troll   57
Muriel Taggert (witch)   60
Muriel Taggert's Ivy Shack   102

N

Nafia   82
Nagi Luna   71
Naiad   47
Navarog   82
Nero (cliff troll)   56
Newel (satyr)   52
Nipsy   28–29
Nymph   46

O

Obsidian Waste   99
Oculus   7
Ogress   48
Old Manor   103
Olloch the Glutton   72
Orogoro   73

P

Peryton   49
Phantom   49
Phoenix   50
Pixie   29
Pixie Cocoon   9
Potions   10
Precious Figurines   12

Q

Quiet Box   12

R

Rain Stick   13
Ranticus   83
Raxtus   83
Register, the   97
Revenant   51
Rio Branco   99
River Troll   58
Roc   51

S

Safe Hut   90
Sage's Gauntlets   13
Sands of Sanctity   7
Satyr   51
Sentinel, the   54
Seven Kingdoms of the Nipsies   104
Shadow Charmer   52
Shrine to the Fairy Queen   104
Shrinking potion   11
Siletta   84
Silver Arrow   14
Singing Sisters   53
Sirrush   54
Skinwalker   54
Slaggo (goblin)   32
Smoke Grenades   14
Society of the Evening Star, the   111
Sphinx   54
Steppe Giant   31
Stingbulb   43
Sunstone   14
Swamp Hag   54

T

Tauran Maze ❧ 105
Tents ❧ 15
Thief's Net ❧ 15
Thronis (giant) ❧ 31
Thylacine ❧ 55
Totem Wall, the ❧ 55
Transdimensional Transporters ❧ 15
Translocator ❧ 7
Troll ❧ 56

U

Udnar (mountain troll) ❧ 57
Umite ❧ 58
Umite Wax ❧ 16
Unicorn ❧ 58–59

V

Valley of the Four Hills, the ❧ 105
Vasilis ❧ 16
Viola (milch cow) ❧ 44–45
Voorsh (goblin) ❧ 32

W

Whirligig ❧ 60
Whisperhound ❧ 60
White Mesh ❧ 16
Witch ❧ 60
Wizard Slime ❧ 61
Wizards ❧ 109
Wraith ❧ 61
Wyrmroost ❧ 89
Wyvern ❧ 62

Y

Yowie ❧ 62

Z

Zogo (dwarf) ❧ 24
Zombie ❧ 63
Zorat the Plagueman ❧ 73
Zzyzx ❧ 105–106

THE SEQUEL TO

Fablehaven

Dragonwatch

SERIES

BY

Brandon Mull

❧──────⟨⟩──────❧

BOOK ONE
COMING FALL 2016

VISIT BRANDONMULL.COM

SHADOW
MOUNTAIN